Get Your
Coventry Romances
Home Subscription NOW

And Get These
4 Best-Selling Novels
FREE:

LACEY
by Claudette Williams

THE ROMANTIC WIDOW
by Mollie Chappell

HELENE
by Leonora Blythe

THE HEARTBREAK TRIANGLE
by Nora Hampton

ANGELA

by

Elizabeth Chater

FAWCETT COVENTRY • NEW YORK

To all those friends of
Richard Bennet
who have demanded that
he get the girl

ANGELA

Published by Fawcett Coventry Books, CBS Educational
and Professional Publishing, a division of CBS Inc.

ISBN: 0-449-50268-6

Printed in the United States of America

First Fawcett Coventry printing: February 1982

10 9 8 7 6 5 4 3 2 1

Chapter 1

ANGELA huddled down beside her mother's old trunk in the attic, too frightened and filled with pain to cry. It had been over a year since her stepfather had beaten her, and the shock of this suddenly renewed cruelty had her trembling as much as the actual hurt. She had escaped his room through the unconscious intervention of the new butler, who had come to inform his master that a brace of fine gentlemen awaited him in the smaller drawing room. Mr. Loring went at once, with a single, baleful glance at the girl.

Angela had run blindly up the stairs to the dusty old attics, scene of some happy childhood hours, sure that that was the last place her well-dressed, complacent stepfather would think of looking for her, since he had never bothered to climb up the narrow, wooden stairway to explore the boxes of fading keepsakes and treasures of the man he had succeeded.

Soon after his marriage to Angela's widowed mother, Mr. Gilles Loring had ordered that everything which reminded his new wife of her former husband must be banished to the attics. "Only in order that you may the sooner forget your grief and begin to enjoy life again, my love," he had said smoothly. "You are Mrs. Gilles Loring now, Marian, and you must never forget it."

As a sensitive fifteen-year-old, Angela had mistrusted her stepfather's smooth self-confidence, and had privately told her mamma that she was not willing to forget the father who had been so wonderful a friend and companion to a growing girl. Mamma had agreed, but her subsequent tears had flowed so painfully that Angela resolved on the spot never to repeat her plea that Father be lovingly remembered in the new family.

Neither Angela nor her mother at first realized what sort of man had replaced the laughing, reckless Denzil Swann, who had killed himself riding in an impromptu, midnight steeplechase with a troop of his boon companions. Gilles Loring was of quite another stripe, a big, heavyset, well-groomed man, who laughed heartily without real mirth, who rode well but without the dash and skill of hell-for-leather Denzil. Indeed, while looking every inch a man's man, Loring preferred to spend his days restoring the neglected estates of Swanholme to their former glory.

"Moderation in all things, my love," he instructed his new wife, "and good, constructive building for the future. We must present a better image to our neighbors than that of a harum-scarum couple continually on the fret for new sensations!"

Angela, who had overheard the remark, took it as a cut at her beloved father, and flamed into a fine rage. The result of this display of temper was the first of many beatings she received from her stepfather. In spite of Marian's anguished pleading, Loring took the girl to his study and whipped her soundly with a small flexible cane. Angela refused to cry, and her aroused stepfather finally was forced to desist when the girl fainted at his feet.

He never beat her as savagely again, for the servants had overheard Marian's frantic appeals, and the story spread throughout the neighborhood.

It appeared that the approval of his neighbors was indeed of prime importance to Mr. Gilles Loring. He had been, it became known, the distant relative and estate manager of a northern nobleman before he came to Averly village—for reasons of health, he always explained with his hearty laugh, as though challenging anyone to find him other than superbly fit. He was in truth a fine figure of a man, and

Marian Swann, widowed a year and quite helpless to manage the comfortable estate her husband had left her, was pathetically eager to accept first his advice, and later, his offer of marriage.

It was not long until he was much more respected in the county than his predecessor had been. Everyone took to saying that Marian had done very well for herself, and that the new master of Swanholme would bring the property up to scratch in a way careless Denzil Swann had never even bothered to attempt. It was also noted, in passing, that it was an added mark of Gilles Loring's integrity that he should expend so much time and energy upon an estate which would become the property of his stepdaughter upon the day she married.

It was at this time, three years after Marian's marriage, that two things happened which changed the rest of Angela's life. The first of these was the introduction into the household at Swanholme of Mr. Vivian Nellis, son of Gilles's sister. This finicking young exquisite was a Londoner, and quite prepared to tell anyone who would listen about the advantages of life in the Metropolis, and of the fine figure he himself cut in the Ton. This elegant Tulip caused many a smothered smile among the stolid, worthy squires and their ladies, the more so because his uncle Gilles, while making excuses for the lad's youthful folly, was also seen to disguise a grin.

"The boy'll be someone youthful for Angela to go about with," Gilles said frequently, his heavy, good-humored face looking solemn. It was true there was a dearth of young people in the district, the offspring of the county's more eminent families being either too young or too old to be suitable companions for an eighteen-year-old female.

It had also become known somehow in the community that poor Loring was finding Denzil's daughter quite a handful. Persons who had been used to consider Angela a charming, happy girl were beginning to wonder how poor Marian managed to put up with her endless whims and ill humors, and to admire her stepfather for his firm but kindly authority. Not that anyone was treated to the sight of one of the temper tantrums they came to hear of, but the rumors began to circulate all the same. They were reinforced by the obvious fading of Marian's fragile beauty, and the new lines of tension and distress which daily appeared on that sad face. Since the bluff and hearty Loring was demonstrably a devoted husband, never allowing his wife to appear without his assiduous attendance, the trouble must be caused by Angela, who seldom appeared at all in society.

Several of the older servants at Swanholme had been lately retired to excellent almshouses, or if they had relatives, were shipped off to them with a generous pension, word of which seemed to percolate into the general knowledge through the same mysterious channels as had the information about Angela's increasing recalcitrance. When Gilles began to say hopefully that perhaps young Nellis, for all his London airs and fads, might bring the girl out and make her happier with her lot in their quiet corner of the world, there was a distinct feeling of admiration and even pity for this good-hearted stepfather, and a growing annoyance at the chit who was causing her poor mother and this good man so much heartache.

To Angela, as to her bewildered, frightened mother, the passing months had seemed to lock them into a nightmare which only they were aware of. The coming of Vivian Nellis seemed, at first, a most fortunate occurrence, since Gilles relaxed his strict supervision of their every action, and, indeed, proposed quite jovially that his dear wife should arrange a series of small dinner parties to introduce their guest to the neighborhood.

"For I know, my love," and he bent his quelling smile upon his trembling wife, "that even with the new servants I have hired to replace those hopelessly antiquated fuddy-duddies, you could never manage a large party in the lamentable state of your health. So I shall draw up the guest lists, and instruct the servants, and your daughter may write out the invitations for you—if she will?" and he turned that complacent smile upon Angela. "Will you condescend to help your poor mother, my dear?"

"You know I shall be only too happy to help her—but she is quite capable of writing a few dinner invitations—or of planning a dinner larger than these! When my father was alive, she often—"

"But your father is dead now, is he not? And your mother prefers to be guided by my judgment, in this as in all other matters. Is this not so, my love?" Gilles took Marian's arm in his big hand and slowly applied pressure, grinning the while.

Marian looked as though she were about to faint. Angela thought for one desperate moment of flying at her stepfather with furious fists, but the sight of her mother's whitening face stopped her.

"I'll do it at once," the girl said dully. "Will— may my mother come to tell me the names?"

Gilles looked down at his wife's face and lifted his eyebrows, as though Angela had said nothing and he still awaited a reply to his question.

"Yes!" Marian gasped, trembling.

"Yes, *what*, my love?" persisted her husband.

"Yes, I will be guided by your judgment, Gilles," Marian swayed in his grasp.

"I thought you might be," said Gilles gently,

releasing her arm, where red marks stood out against the white skin. "Now, I think you should rest for a while. I shall accompany you to our room—my love." He smiled at Angela as he led her mother out of the room.

For the next few weeks the reception rooms and the kitchens at Swanholme bustled with activity, and the gentry of the area came to meet Mr. Loring's nephew and be amused. Angela was glad for the opportunity to be busy and to meet many of her father's old friends, but she began to sense a restraint in their attitude toward her which hurt her and drove her deeper into that sense of nightmare which seemed to be engulfing her. The unhappy climax to this new situation came with the rather bitter little comment from one of her mother's oldest friends. Drawing the girl aside when the ladies retired after one of the small, formal dinners, old Mrs. Bothwell said, "Angela, I think I should urge you to try to curb your rebellious spirits just a little. Your mother is not in the best of health, and I cannot think your constant fussing at her can do anything but harm!"

Angela was so startled by this unwarranted attack that she stood stupidly staring at the older woman. "But I have not—" she began.

Mrs. Bothwell was not finished. "It is well known," she went on, "that your father never considered her feelings when *he* was alive. Now she has a chance of happiness with Gilles, it is time *you* thought of someone other than yourself. Try not to worry her, my dear, and we shall soon see the roses back in her pale cheeks!" With a final, minatory smile, she went over to join a chattering group of her peers, leaving the girl to watch her mother closely for the rest of the interminable evening.

She was forced to admit that her mother was not well. Her beauty had always been of a delicate, fragile nature, but of late months it had become almost transparent in its pallor. Heavy purple shadows surrounded the once-sparkling eyes; the soft lips trembled and worked nervously in a constant, placating smile.

This nervous grimace became even more noticeable when Mr. Loring led the group of loud-talking men into the drawing room for coffee and liqueurs. He went to stand beside Marian, and it was plain even to Angela that he took her glass of cordial gently from her and placed it upon the table. Then with a cautionary hand upon her arm, he led her the circuit of their guests in a smoothly social exercise.

In the meantime, Vivian was basking in the approval of a few young wives of local importance who professed themselves more than eager to hear the lastest on-dits from the Beau Monde, and descriptions of the most outstanding costumes and coiffures to be seen there. The flattered youth discoursed willingly upon trends and fads, delighting his feminine audience with his expertise as much as he had amused their husbands with his finicking ways.

Vivian had not expected to stay so long in the country, but his uncle's surprising generosity, as much as the adulation of a few young matrons, was reconciling him to the extended visit. He even tried out his hand at a little patronizing flirtation with his uncle's stepdaughter, finding her pretty enough, with her soft dark hair and wide gray eyes, although sadly lacking in sophisticated coquetry or town bronze. He might have tired of this game sooner, had not her total indifference to the lures he was casting out provoked him to the point of resolving to make her a willing captive of his charm.

Tonight Angela quite ignored his posturings. Her whole concern was for her mother, perceived to be so terribly fallen off. Angela could not believe that this transformation could be the result of anything she had done; however, she determined to ask her mother point-blank what was troubling her. With this intent, she waited until the last guest had gone, and then, before her expansive stepfather had quite completed playing the genial host at the front door, slipped over to where her mother stood by the table, sipping desperately at a small glass of liqueur.

"Dearest Mother," Angela said softly, "is anything the matter?"

Marian started and slopped some of the cordial upon the table. "Matter? What do you mean?"

"Mrs. Bothwell informed me, in her usual style," the girl essayed a grin, "that you were far from well. She intimated that I might be to blame. Dear Mamma, *pray* tell me what I am doing to hurt you!"

Marian swayed slightly, and Angela was forced to admit that her mother had had too frequent recourse to the liqueur decanter. "You, my dearest child? *You* have done nothing which would hurt me . . . nor ever could! Oh, if only I had not—"

"If only you had not what, my love?" prodded the voice which Angela found so hateful. Her stepfather strolled into the room. "A most successful dinner party, my dear wife," Gilles said in a self-congratulatory tone. "Quite the best we have given to date, I think. And now you must come to bed, my love. Rest, that is what you need. Complete rest. Am I not right?"

"Yes, Gilles," agreed Marian dully, but her frightened gaze sought out her daughter's anxious one with an unmistakable warning.

For once, Gilles did not seem satisfied with her submission. "I believe it is time we had a little talk about Angela's future," he said softly, taking her arm. "Tonight, I think."

"Oh, Gilles, I am so very tired tonight!" whispered Marian. "Could we not postpone the—the talk until tomorrow—please?"

Gilles Loring smiled and led her from the room, quite ignoring the wide-eyed girl.

"Oh, no, we'll have our little talk tonight. And then afterwards, I'll see if I can't give you something to help you to rest."

When they had passed beyond her sight into the hall, Angela roused herself to follow them. She was prey to the most alarming apprehensions. Her attention directed by Mrs. Bothwell to the extreme fragility of her mother's appearance, she castigated herself for not noticing it long before. Had her mother been looking so unwell all these months? How could she have failed to notice? What could she do now? Rigorously though she searched her conscience, she could not find any action or speech of hers which might have reduced her mother to this state.

Suddenly making up her mind to demand an answer, she ran lightly up the stairs and paused outside the master bedroom. Gently she tried the handle. The door was locked! Hovering in the hallway, undecided whether to knock or to allow the matter to rest until the following day, the girl heard, through the thick panel of the door, the faintest sound of a despairing cry.

Mother!

Almost without thinking, Angela ran down the hallway and slipped into the dressing room which served the master bedroom. It was dark there, but a thin slit of light declared that the door into her parent's bedroom was slightly ajar. Without scruple, the girl crept over and positioned herself against the wall beside the opened door.

The first voice she heard was Loring's.

"—past time that your daughter admitted her responsibilities and accepted Vivian's offer—"

Angela went rigid. *Vivian had made her no offer. He didn't even like her! What little time he favored her with his company, he spent in boasting about his triumphs and conquests at Almack's.*

When Angela was able to listen again, it was to hear her mother's despairing voice.

"You are right in saying that Angela should marry soon, Gilles, although I cannot agree that she is quite on the shelf at eighteen. Perhaps we all might accompany Vivian back to London, request your sister to sponsor Angela into the Beau Monde . . . give her a chance at a suitable marriage?"

"I have decided she is to marry Vivian." The statement brooked no argument.

Still, Marian found the courage to protest. "But your nephew shows no real interest in her—no *tendresse*—"

Gilles's coarse, mocking laughter cut short Marian's pitiful effort at resistance.

"Do you claim there are other, more eligible *partis* clamoring after her here at Averly? I

17

have not *quite* had to barricade the house against hordes of importunate suitors, in spite of the fact that her damned father made sure she gets the lot when she marries! And as for London— Are you ready to be turned into the street as soon as some puffed-up, stiff-rumped lordling gets his perfumed fingers on her fortune and Swanholme?"

"Is *that* what irks you?" said Marian, her voice revealing shocked comprehension. Then, in a tone almost of horror, she continued, "Then it is all *your* doing! Mavis Bothwell told me tonight of some of the rumors you have caused to be set abroad against Angela—vicious lies!"

There was a pregnant pause.

Angela felt a grue of fear and loathing chill her flesh. What reprisal would Gilles Loring make to such a charge? The answer was not long in coming.

With his coarse laugh, Gilles said triumphantly, "Yes, I have fooled all the gape-seeds in this smug little community rather neatly! Diddled the dupes! And you, my love, were the easiest of all! But having got your comfortable little fortune for myself, you can hardly expect me to throw it all into the capacious pockets of the first fortune hunter who fancies it. No, my love, my stupid nephew shall marry the chit, and hare back to his fleshpots with my blessing and a cozy pension warming his wallet, while you

18

and I shall continue as we have begun—*very nicely*, don't you agree?"

There was a muffled gasp from Marian, followed by a pleading whimper.

This was too much for the horrified girl in the dressing room. She flung the door wide, and stormed into the room.

"What are you doing to my mother, you beast?"

"Oh, Angela," moaned the disheveled Marian, "please go—at once!"

Gilles Loring took his time in releasing the cruel grip he had on his wife. Marian slumped to the bed, weeping silently. Angela drew a shaking breath and made the first frantic plea which came to her mind.

"If I sign the whole over to you, will you forget this absurd design of marrying me off to your horrid nephew, and let my mother and me go?"

Gilles laughed, but his eyes were narrow with fury. "Let you go where, wench? To sleep in the hedges and whine your pitiful tale to anyone who would listen? What do you take me for? I have not spent three years of my life in this narrow-minded hamlet building a reputation, just to throw it all away on such a totty-headed scheme. No, brat, you'll marry my nephew and then stay on here with your mother and me when I send the fribble back to his London drawing rooms." He grinned at her mockingly. "Our good neighbors may whisper, but they'll commiserate with you upon your absentee husband, and they will admire you for your devotion to your poor, ailing mother."

Meeting Gilles's slyly triumphant gaze, Angela began to see the whole scope of his cold-blooded, greedy plan. And suddenly his physical presence became so repugnant, so terrifying, to her that she turned and raced for the door in a panic. She had forgotten that her stepfather had locked it. While she was twisting frantically at the key, his iron grip descended upon her shoulder. She found herself dragged round to face him, but instead of detaining her, Gilles turned the key and invited her to go with a wide, mocking smile.

Casting one worried glance at her mother, now huddled on the floor at the foot of the bed with her hands over her face, Angela ran out into the hallway. She had reached the top of the stairs when a burly figure moved to intercept her. It was Gilles's new butler, Danvers. The fellow did not touch her, but he placed himself in front of her so that she could not descend the stairs.

Angela's hand flew to stifle the involuntary cry she would have uttered. Danvers said nothing, but glanced above her head toward his master, still standing in the door of the bedroom.

"You may escort Miss Angela back here,"

Gilles said. "I believe her mother has something to say to her."

Without waiting for Danvers to compel her, Angela turned and retraced her way to the master bedroom.

Chapter 2

GILLES Loring summoned his nephew and his stepdaughter to his study the following morning. Angela opened the door slowly, reluctant to face again that complacent, mocking stare with which he had regarded her and her mother the previous night as Marian pleaded for her daughter to obey her stepfather. Whatever Gilles had intended to say to her in greeting this morning was lost, however, as young Nellis arrived in a fine fret.

He began at once to complain in a high, artificial tone, as he pushed past the startled girl without apology or recognition.

"Stap me, Nunky," he said, at his most affected, "this is the outside of enough! A man scarcely gets his eyeballs open in this bucolic retreat before he's summoned to a family Confabulation! It had better be something pretty important to drag me from my bedchamber before I've got my cravat properly tied!"

"It's important," his uncle said quietly. "It concerns your marriage to—your cousin."

The expression of surprise and dawning alarm upon Vivian's pasty countenance might have amused Angela at any other time. As it was, she suspected that her own features revealed a matching discomfort. Young Nellis was stammering.

"M-m-marriage, Uncle Gilles? Y-y-you d-did say *marriage*?"

"To Angela," Gilles explained slowly, as to an idiot, "my stepdaughter. Your stepcousin, I suppose we might say." He held up one hand to forestall further incoherent babbling. "Girl's an heiress." Then he gave his mocking smile as Vivian abruptly ceased objecting and turned to look at the girl with interest.

"Thought that would make you change your tune," Loring said succinctly. "I've a few papers here for you to sign. There's a comfortable sum of money which I shall pay you monthly—"

Vivian frowned pettishly. "My friends in London!" he pouted. "What will they say when I return from a simple rustication in the country with a wife in tow? No, it really won't fadge, sir! Miss Angela is a—a pleasant enough girl, but she's not—that is, well, sir," with a sideways glance at the girl, "I'm known to set a pretty high standard, even with my flirts, and I don't think—"

"That statement is correct, at least," snapped

24

Gilles, whose patience with any folly other than his own was short indeed. "You don't think! You may call this little visit to the country a simple rustication, but my sister tells me a different story! One step ahead of your creditors, Vivian, and your father quite unable, or at least unwilling, to raise the recruits for you! It might be worth your while to consider my proposition."

"But I don't want to be married!" whined Vivian. "My mamma did not hint of anything so—so *final* when she sent me down here!" He turned to face the girl. "Pray do not take a pet, Miss Angela! It is not that I find you repulsive, I assure you—" Gilles gave a snort of laughter, "—but I have no wish to tie myself up so soon. And as for living in the country—" The horrified revulsion on his pasty face was almost ludicrous.

"But you would not have to live in the country, Vivian," vouchsafed his uncle. "Nor would you have to drag to London an unacceptable bride. Angela will stay here with her mother, whose health is causing us both a good deal of concern." Gilles favored the girl with a long, warning look. "I cannot really guarantee her continued well-being if her daughter deserts her at this juncture." Under that glare, Angela's face became even paler.

Vivian Nellis hesitated. He had, as he said, no real desire to enter the wedded state. Getting leg-shackled was a matter of ribald jest in his circle; none but the unwary or the financially hard-pressed were caught in Parson's mousetrap. But his circumstances, as his uncle had pointed out, were very much down pin, and looked to be in a fair way to becoming disastrous if he could not find means to come about. Perhaps, if the monthly sum of money Uncle Gilles had mentioned was liberal enough . . . Taking his courage in both hands, Vivian faced his tempter.

"How much?"

Gilles grinned. "I like a man who can go straight to the heart of the matter," he said approvingly. "One thousand pounds when you sign the register, and fifty a month as long as you stay in harness. Well?"

Visions of largesse warmed Vivian's heart. He nodded decisively. "I'm your man, Nunky," he agreed.

"No!" said Angela desperately.

Neither man accorded her the courtesy of a glance or a word. Gilles was pouring two generous measures of whiskey. Vivian, a little pale, was at pains to convince himself that he had made the correct decision: he was listing the things he would be able to do in Town with a nice little steady income. "For you must have heard from my mamma that my father is the greatest nipcheese in London! He expects his only child to exist upon a miserable pittance,

26

yet he demands that I associate with members of the Ton! Oh!" as an unpleasant thought struck him, "what shall I tell my father about this marriage?"

"Tell him nothing," advised Gilles, handing over one of the filled glasses. "I should trust your mamma to deal with the matter, if I were you."

Angela came toward them, her small face set with anger. "I *will not* be ignored! You speak of me as though I were not here. You settle my future as though I had no say in it!"

Gilles turned to her at last. "You have no say," he informed her. "You were told last night what I intended to do." His eyes scanned her face almost avidly. "Do you tell me you are wishing to change your mind? Perhaps we should go up to see your mother. She may be persuaded of the wisdom of advising you to obey me."

The big man moved out to the hall and began to ascend the stairway. After one moment of indecision, Angela ran after him. By the time she reached her parent's bedroom, the door was securely locked. The girl ran to the dressing room door, only to discover that it, too, was sealed against her. She ran back to the door of the master bedroom, bent close, and leaned her ear against the panel.

In a moment she heard a sharp cry of pain. She set her teeth. There was a deep-voiced rumble, as though Gilles were making some sort of harangue, and then, more clearly, a second sharp cry, almost a shriek. Angela began to batter on the door with her small fists.

"Oh, stop, I pray you! I will marry Vivian! I will!"

Chapter 3

THE following day there occurred the second of the events which were to change Angela's life so drastically.

She had not been permitted to enter her mother's room the previous night, nor had her mother emerged from her seclusion. Gilles, however, had come out into the hall soon after the girl had made her impassioned plea outside the door. He had closed and locked it behind him, refusing to allow a glimpse of his wife in spite of the girl's anguished requests. He had taken one of her hands in his and seized her chin in the other, forcing her face up to meet his scrutiny.

"Well, Miss, have you decided to accept my decision?" he demanded.

"Yes, yes!" sobbed the girl. "If you will not hurt my mother any more!"

"Hurt your mother? What can you be talking about, you silly child? Your mother is my dear wife, and as such, it is her duty to obey me in all things. If she does not, it is *my* duty to . . . instruct her in the error of her ways . . . " He gave Angela his mirthless grin.

"But it was I who—who defied you," protested the girl.

"It is usually considered to be the mother's fault if the child behaves badly," her stepfather informed her smugly. "So I must punish the one responsible for the disobedience."

"I shall not disobey you again," promised the girl.

"It is to be hoped you will not, for Marian's sake. It really pains me to have to administer such punishment to her in her frail condition. I trust you will remember that?"

By the following day, Marian had still not emerged from her room. Gilles had her meals brought to the dressing room on a tray, and served her himself, which caused the female members of the staff to think Mrs. Loring a pretty lucky woman to be so cossetted. Her absence seemed to go otherwise unremarked by anyone but Angela. Gilles smilingly refused to let her visit her mamma, telling her that her recalcitrance had quite unnerved her maternal parent.

"She will go on famously if she is let to rest," he said with his usual bonhomie. Angela had a queer, disturbing notion that there was something quite cold and alien under that habitual wide smile, and resolved to find a way to see her

30

mother as soon as possible. The only other key to the bedroom was the master key carried by Danvers, and hung at night in the butler's pantry. Angela knew there was no use appealing to Danvers—he was Loring's creature. Perhaps she could insist that she needed her mother's advice about her trousseau?

The household was agog with preparations for the reception which would announce the engagement of Miss Angela Swann, spinster of this parish, to Mr. Vivian Nellis, bachelor, of London. Vivian, meanwhile, was loudly lamenting that he had not brought his finest raiment to Averly, having felt it would be out of place in so rural a setting. His uncle assured him jovially that he would cut a damned sharp swathe with the finery he had brought.

"Wear that pink and green coat you favored us with the other night," he advised. "I'll wager a pony you'll strike 'em dumb with that!" Then, wearied by his nephew's endless babble about his clothing, Gilles suggested that they ride out along the Penzance road and exercise the horses. When Vivian protested that he had not the urge to go hacking across country, his uncle informed him that he was getting a potbelly just like Prinny's, unbecoming in so young a man. This threat was enough to persuade Mr. Nellis to accompany his uncle on the suggested excursion.

Soon after they had cantered off, Mrs. Bothwell was announced, to see Mrs. Loring. Marian's old friend was a high stickler; she invariably paid her duty calls within forty-eight hours of being entertained, to thank her hostess with meticulous formality. Since the master was absent, and Danvers was in the wine cellar reviewing the possibilities for the engagement party, the footman perforce summoned Miss Angela to do the honors.

Angela greeted her mother's friend with what the latter regarded as excessive enthusiasm.

"Oh, I am so happy you have come!" she began, on a breathless note. "I have not been permitted to visit Mamma for two days! No one but my stepfather sees her! I am sure she is not well!"

Mrs. Bothwell took a calming attitude.

"Perhaps Marian herself requested that she be left to regain her strength in quiet? She has declined very noticeably this last six-month."

"Yes, but what is wrong?" fretted Angela. "Why will not Mr. Loring call in Dr. Slomayn? Why is no one permitted to visit Mamma but my stepfather? I beg of you, Mrs. Bothwell, for the love you bear my mother, come with me to see her now!"

Reluctantly the good dame allowed herself to be persuaded. Without attracting the notice of any of Mr. Loring's servants, the two women mounted the stairway and proceeded along the corridor to the master bedroom. The door was locked as usual. Angela tried it gently to prove her point to her mother's old friend. Then, followed by a very sober-looking Mrs. Bothwell, the girl led the way to the door of the dressing room. By some oversight, this had not been locked by Gilles in his haste to get Vivian into the saddle. The two women entered quietly.

The first thing they beheld was the morning's breakfast tray, quite untouched. Angela moved to the inner door which led into the bedroom. Quietly she turned the doorknob. The door swung open.

All the blinds were drawn. The room was in almost complete darkness. There was an odor of sickness heavy in the close atmosphere. On the bed, neatly covered to the chin, lay the thin body of Marian Loring, so frail that she scarcely raised the coverlet. Mrs. Bothwell caught her breath sharply as she hurried over to her friend's side.

"Marian!" she said. "What is wrong? What can I do for you?"

Marian's eyes were set in dark purple bruises in her pallid face. Slowly the lids drew up; slowly she peered at her old friend.

"Mavis," she whispered. "Where is Angela? Is she—safe?"

Not stopping at the moment to wonder at the odd nature of the latter question, Mavis held out her hand and drew the girl toward the bed. "She is here, dear Marian. She has been so alarmed for you—puzzled that you had not summoned her to attend you—"

"I could not let the child see me like—this," whispered the sick woman. "I—that is, Gilles . . . forbade her to come to me . . ."

"Do not try to talk now, my dear," said Mrs. Bothwell. "We shall get Dr. Slomayn to come at once. I cannot think why Mr. Loring has not done so long since!"

"You must not," breathed the sick woman. "Gilles has sworn to beat me again if anyone sends for the doctor—"

"To beat you!" exclaimed her horrified friend. "Do you tell me your husband *beats you?*"

In desperate haste the woman in the bed thrust herself upright to a seated position. The coverlet fell from her, revealing bruises which caused Mavis Bothwell to suck in her breath and Angela to cry out in horrified revulsion. "You must say nothing—do nothing!" gasped Marian. "You have no notion of what he will do to me—and to Angela—if anything becomes known of my condition. I implore you—say nothing!"

Her great eyes held them, begged for their assurance of silence.

Angela, on her knees beside the bed, was crying softly as she kissed her mother's thin hand. Mavis Bothwell stared hard at the desperate countenance before her.

34

"Promise you will never breathe a word of this!" demanded Marian.

Mavis Bothwell hesitated. It went against every feeling, every principle, to make that promise, yet she knew beyond doubt that whatever punishment her friend's husband administered to his wife and daughter, he was legally within his rights and could not be called to account. Marian had warned that any interference on her friend's part would only result in further torment. She nodded reluctantly.

"As you wish, my dear, but I should like to consult the doctor—"

At the end of her frail strength, Marian fell back onto the pillows. "You will only add to my sufferings," she whispered.

"Very well. I promise. But what can I do for you? You can not be allowed to continue in this state."

"Gilles wishes me to attend the wedding. If Angela is obedient to him, he says he will not whip me again before then."

Mavis Bothwell set her jaw. It was an impasse, a situation from which there was no possible escape, and she knew it. Gilles Loring had all the authority and excellent means of controlling both women, vulnerable as they were through their love for one another. And she herself could not even inform the community of the monster they had welcomed in their midst! Still, Marian must be reassured.

"I promise to say nothing. I know Angela will do exactly as her stepfather directs, to save you further pain. Dear Marian, can you not try to sip a little wine, or broth, or take a glass of warm milk? You must recruit your strength for the wedding, you know!"

Angela's great gray eyes were fixed on her mother's face. The sick woman essayed a smile.

"Just a bowl of bread and warm milk, dearest," she answered her daughter's unspoken plea. "You remember the way I used to make it for you . . ."

Angela rose and ran from the room. Marian's eyes had closed again. Tears ran down Mavis Bothwell's seamed face, but she said nothing, merely held the thin hand of her old friend.

That night, alone in the newly locked room, while her husband and his nephew drank themselves into a stupor in the dining room, and were left there, sleeping, by the servants, Marian Loring slipped as quietly from life as she could have wished. Gilles discovered her body the next morning when he brought her breakfast tray into the bedroom he had failed to reach the night before.

Chapter 4

ANGELA was summoned again to her stepfather's study that morning. The first thing she saw was the slender, flexible cane with which he had been wont to punish her, but which she had not seen for a year. It gave her anguish to suspect that, during that interminable year, her mother had been accepting the punishment which Gilles had formerly given Marian's daughter. Had it indeed been so? Was that the reason Gilles had stopped beating her? She raised eyes in which hatred warred with grief to scrutinize her stepfather's face. It lacked its normal ruddy hue; the complacent smile was missing.

"I have some news for you," Gilles Loring began with less assurance than usual.

Angela, apprehensive, said nothing.

"Your mother is dead."

The girl frowned, shook her head. What new devil's trick was this? Had Gilles decided upon a different kind of torture? "No." She denied the possibility that he spoke truth.

"She must have died during the night. She has been sickly for a long time—no fit wife for a healthy man—as I was often forced to remind her. But I do not intend my plans to be thwarted by any maudlin display of sentiment. We shall proceed with the wedding as I arranged, only now we shall be able to dispense with the expense and bother of a big county affair. Just a quiet ceremony here at Swanholme, with only the required number of witnesses. People will quite understand that a newly bereaved husband cannot wish for an elaborate show." His composure was returning; he managed one of his mirthless smiles. "I shall have your mother buried quietly tomorrow. Then the day after, you and Vivian will be wed without fuss or palaver."

"Are you insane?" gasped the girl. "What will be the attitude among the neighbors you are always so desirous of impressing, when they observe your unseemly haste?" The shock of his matter-of-fact announcement and cold-blooded program momentarily insulated Angela from her own grief. At this instant, she had room only for horror at her stepfather's callous insensitivity. "You are despicable! The whole county will know you for what you are!"

"Indeed?" His complacence quite restored, Gilles picked up the slender cane. "I had antici-

pated that you might wish to dispute my deci
sion, so I am prepared to—to reason with you."
He moved around from behind Denzil's desk
and approached the girl, who stood frozen with
terror, staring at him. "You have not shed a
single tear for your dear mamma, have you, my
child? Perhaps I had better remedy that sad
lack in you."

The next few minutes were an agony for the
girl. Weakened as her spirit was by the news
of her mother's death, she was not able to resist
the pain of the beating. Her tears flowed; she
sobbed and moaned under the blows. Gilles
finally flung down the cane.

"It is good to see that you have the relief of
tears," he smiled. "Now get up to your room and
put on black clothing for the look of the thing. I
shall arrange the funeral at once."

It was then that Angela fled to the attics, to
which limbo Gilles had banished all mementos
of his predecessor and where he himself had
never been known to come, and huddled down
beside Marian's old trunk, so often used when
they accompanied Denzil on one of his impromptu visits to London. Here Angela wept
for the beloved mother who had borne in silence
the punishments which otherwise might have
been inflicted upon her only child. After a long
time the girl's tears ceased to flow. She sat up
and peered around her through reddened, puffed
eyelids. It came into her mind that the life

Gilles had planned for her, while just bearable as long as she had her mother's presence to strengthen her, was a nightmare impossibility now. To be alone in the house with Gilles Loring and his servants! Better to go to London with her foppish new husband than to allow herself to be sequestered in a lonely house at the mercy of a monster of cruelty!

Angela squared her shoulders, accepting the new burden. She would go with Vivian Nellis when he left for London. Of course he cared nothing for her, would feel her to be an encumbrance, but she could promise him that she would never interfere with his pleasures, stay completely in the background, if only he would take her with him away from Swanholme!

Then she caught her breath in a frightened inhalation. It would not fadge! Vivian was weak. He would do whatever his uncle bade him. His bribe and stipend depended upon that! It was too much to hope that Gilles would permit the girl who owned the estate he coveted to get beyond his reach! Too many things could happen once his stepdaughter arrived in London, free of his control. With a fearful sinking of spirit, Angela realized that if she were ever to be free of Gilles Loring, it must be before she was locked into a marriage with his nephew. But how? The house servants were all loyal to Loring—they were his creatures. Had he kept any of the old retainers who might be expected to have some affection for their former master's daughter? Frantically she considered the roster: Gilles had brought his own groom with him, and Botts had found his own ostlers and stableboys. But wait! Old Beamish was still here! He had saddled her mare for her the last time she rode, and had lingered to phrase an awkward sentence or two about old times. Beamish! If she could get to him, arrange for a horse, run away!

A moment's careful consideration revealed the numerous flaws in that scheme. Unless she left with just what she stood in, her departure from the stables with luggage would be witnessed and reported. And when the horse did not return, Old Beamish would be punished, sent away, and he had no place to go and no one to care if he lived or died. Could she put at risk the security of an old man? Angela drew a long, shuddering breath. It was time, at almost eighteen years old, she told herself, that she began to use the intelligence she possessed. There must be a better, safer plan. She had made up her mind to escape. First she would need clothing. Easing her aching body up from the floor, she opened her mother's old trunk.

A waft of lavender came to her nostrils. Folded neatly on top were several costumes, perhaps outmoded, but gay and pretty and in good repair. They had been new when Marian married Gilles, but he had told his wife he didn't approve of

41

them. She had docilely packed them away and purchased, under his supervision, dresses he deemed more suitable for Gilles Loring's wife.

Angela doffed her crumpled, torn woolen dress and scrambled into a riding habit with long, draped skirt and a military flair of epaulettes and buttons. It fitted her slender body very well, but the color—a rich, light blue—was so noticeable that Angela knew she could be easily traced by it. Then she found the somber black dress, cloak and bonnet which Marian had bought to wear to the funeral of Denzil's Aunt Alys, and had never worn again.

The girl seized upon this funereal garb with satisfaction. It was dowdy and unremarkable. As she draped the voluminous cloak about her slender frame, she felt almost as though Marian was offering her protection for the desperate plan. Slipping her own dusty dress back on, the girl bundled up the black raiment and closed the trunk. Then, about to return to her room, she recalled her favorite memento, the miniature of her parents painted upon ivory. Denzil, young and happy, was smiling widely as he held his young wife in the curve of one strong arm. The miniature had been one of the first things Gilles had banished from the drawing room. Angela ran to the dusty old cabinet in one corner of the attic and found the painting in a drawer. Tucking it into her bosom under her fichu, she made her way to her mother's room without meeting any of the servants.

Marian Swann Loring, fragile and lonely under a fresh counterpane, had in death a look more peaceful and serene than she had worn in life. The long fair hair had been neatly brushed and braided by the doctor's old female assistant who laid out bodies for burial. The thin hands had been crossed upon the breast. Angela bent over and kissed her mother on the cheek. Then, dry-eyed, she crept from the room.

She did not go down to luncheon, but washed away the dust and cobwebs of the attic carefully before she changed into her best underclothing and her Sunday dress. Choosing an old drawstring bag which had belonged to her mother, she filled it with the small keepsakes which were her very own: the miniature, a tiny ring, too small now, given her by Denzil for her tenth birthday, which held a tiny diamond; next followed a change of underclothing, wrapped small, two handkerchieves, and a soft lace fichu which would not wrinkle for being crushed. Then came the lavender soap, the making of which had always been one of Marian's pleasures.

Angela looked around her bedroom carefully, her sorrow-darkened eyes forlorn. So little left to mark the happiness the Swann family had known! She would not be reluctant to leave Swanholme now, for it had been darkened by the greedy shadow of Gilles Loring. Then the girl mocked herself. Reluctant to leave? She would be fortunate indeed if she could manage to get away from the surveillance of Loring and his sycophantic servants!

Where could she go? She had no money for the stagecoach, no relatives or friends who might be willing to shelter her from her legal guardian. Even the redoubtable old Mrs. Bothwell would be unable to protect her, or keep her out of the hands of her stepfather, whose right to control her person was absolute under the law.

Very well, then, she must manage alone. Think! she commanded herself. But that was easier said than done. She began to pace her bedroom floor, concocting and rejecting plan after plan. It was while she was thus engaged that she became aware of another presence in the room. Turning, she beheld Gilles Loring in the act of closing the door behind him. He grinned at her.

"It is all settled, girl. I've just come from a long, encouraging chat with Dr. Slomayn and Parson Quayle. After a few mellowing glasses of run-brandy, they were full of pity for the bereaved husband. I even got Quayle to agree to conduct a wedding between Vivian and you within three days!" he gloated.

"How could you persuade—" choked the girl.

"I presented the idea that my sorrowing daughter needed the protection of a young, ardent husband . . . a change of scene—" he chuckled.

44

It was apparent that her stepfather had enjoyed the brandy as much as had the doctor and the priest. Angela saw a ray of hope in his words.

"A change of scene?" she whispered, her great gray eyes searching his ruddy face.

Gilles barked a laugh. "Don't get your hopes arounsed, girl! When Vivian is ready to leave for London, it will be found that you have an illness—a putrid sore throat, maybe, or a colicky disorder—which will make it quite ineligible for you to set out upon such a tiring journey." He smiled tauntingly. "I am free at last! Free of your wretched, puling mamma, free to look elsewhere for my pleasure . . . to younger, fresher bodies!"

Hypnotized by his triumphant, bulging eyes, Angela felt herself losing consciousness. The room seemed to sway and turn around her, and the light waxed and waned. Surely Gilles could not mean the thing he was implying—could he? She sought to regain control of her senses.

Gilles had turned to the bed and was examining the black garments she had placed there.

"Is that what you intend to rig yourself out in, for the funeral?"

"It is an old dress M-mother wore to Aunt Alys Swann's funeral," she explained.

"Won't do!" Gilles belched. "I can't have all the busybodies in the neighborhood saying I decked you out in your mother's old rags!"

"I have no money to buy anything else—and

no time," the the girl reminded him. "Since you have arranged the funeral for tomorrow."

"It will be late in the afternoon," Gilles told her. "If you go to the village at once—" He scrutinized the pale, desolate face suspiciously. "You look sufficiently mournful to satisfy the quizzies. I'll take you into Averly this afternoon— no, damn it! I have to be here to receive courtesy calls. I'll give you money and send you with Poll. Will you like that plan?" He watched her expression closely.

Angela knew he was testing her, and she deliberately removed from her voice and her face all signs of vitality or rebellion. "Would that not look very odd to the neighbors? Should I not be here with you this afternoon?" Her hands were clenched into white-knuckled fists, but she hid them within the voluminous folds of her woolen skirt. "I'll wear this black dress of Mother's, or one of my Sunday dresses."

"That you will not!" contradicted her stepfather. "You will go with Poll to the village at once!" As she had hoped, his desire to exert his authority over her had led him to demand the very course of action Angela wished to take. Could she manage to escape from the surveillance of Poll, a buxom, hard-eyed brunette with a bold, overfamiliar manner?

"I am still too sore from the beating you gave me to walk so far," objected the girl, daring

46

greatly. "You will have to ask Mrs. Webster to come here. Besides, I have no money."

With a vicious imprecation, Gilles flung a small leather purse at her feet. "You'll walk! And any pain you exhibit will be considered as grief for your dear mother," he said. Then, as she still hesitated, "Pick up the purse, damn you! And I know exactly how much is in it, Miss! You will return whatever the Webster woman does not take. I'll warn Poll to watch every move you make!"

Angela bent her head to disguise the incredulous joy she felt. A full purse! And to go to the village without Gilles's supervision! And, she promised herself grimly, she would even find some way to handle Poll!

Within half an hour Angela, arrayed in her best Sunday costume and closely attended by the aggressive Poll, walked rapidly down the driveway of Swanholme and made her way to the village of Averly. The girl was more fortunate than she had dared to hope. Poll was easily diverted to a close study of feathered bonnets and brightly colored silk scarves. While she tried these on in the outer room which was the cottage's shop and showroom, Angela retired to the bedroom in which Mrs. Webster did her sewing and fitting. After offering her condolences, the sempstress announced that she had a bolt of black silk, which she offered to drape over a gray tabby gown already cut and partly

47

sewed for another customer. "For indeed she's gone to Penzance for a fortnight, and I can stitch up another dress for her before she returns." The old lady gave Angela a searching look. "It's all been very hasty, hasn't it, my dear? Your mother's funeral, and then the wedding?"

Angela stroked the exquisite watered silk with the silvery sheen. She hardly knew how to reply. Her stepfather had so shrewdly consolidated his image as a benevolent, hearty, man's man in the district that it would have been quite impossible for Angela to change the picture with a few words. Instead she shook her head sadly, and offered the good woman the money Gilles had provided—a generous amount, to reinforce his pose of benefactor.

"It's far too much," protested Mrs. Webster.

"I think Mr. Loring wished to recompense you for the trouble you will have in hurrying the dress through," Angela confided with an ingenuous smile. "He also suggested that you might provide Poll with a scarf . . . or something. She has been of great service to him . . . in this crisis."

Mrs. Webster nodded but said nothing, giving the pale-faced girl an old-fashioned look. *Quality* might be fooled by Mr. Gilles Loring, but *she* was not, having sewed for Marian Swann in happier days. She went to her little cash box and took out several pound notes which she pressed into the girl's hand. "I'll bring the dress to you tomorrow morning, my dear child. And I'll let that Poll choose a scarf, and tell her it and your dress required all the money your stepfather sent. She won't blab as long as she has her scarf, and men know nothing about the cost of women's clothing anyway—except to grumble at it!"

Faint with gratitude for the help from this unexpected quarter, Angela thrust the money within her bodice and smiled tremulously at the old woman. Exultation warmed her blood. She had enough now to pay the fare on the stagecoach, if she could manage to get to it without discovery, and maintain herself in some distant town until she could find employment.

Yet as the day waned, hope waned with it. Although he did not question the girl's announcement that Mrs. Webster had required all the money he sent, merely muttering something about cursed village screws, he did not permit Angela to absent herself at all during the rest of the day from his constant surveillance, even detailing Poll to accompany her to her room that night. When Angela was safely in her bed, Poll squirmed to settle her ample frame in a padded armchair.

"Do you have to perch in that uncomfortable roost all night, poor Poll?" queried the girl in a pseudo-pitying, sleepy voice.

Poll uttered a word not commonly to be heard

in a lady's presence. "Yus,————! I've got to pay twice for the present you got me."

"Why not just lock me in and get some rest?" Angela offered idly.

"He'd have my hide for it, your dad would," averred the woman.

"Good night, then," murmured Angela, and pretended to drift off to sleep. But Poll's vigilance did not seem to be relaxing, and a weary Angela dropped off with freedom no closer than it had ever been.

The following morning, all was bustle to prepare the house for the visits which would follow the short church ceremony. Danvers had brought up the finest brandies from the cellar; the maids were kept busy preparing pasties and small cakes for the wake. Through it all, Gilles hovered above his kingdom like a tyrant, alert for any sign of disobedience. Angela, forced to bide her time, donned the hastily pulled-together mourning gown and spent her time trying to entertain the very bored and petulant Vivian. That callow youth was already fretting to return to London, and was in no very lenient frame of mind. Still, Angela managed to keep him sweet so that he did not let his rancor become too evident to the neighbors who called to commiserate with the bereaved family. That her yeoman efforts had not gone unremarked the girl learned when the door had finally closed on the last of the guests.

"Thank God that's over!" whined Vivian, pouring himself a generous drink.

"Thank your future wife that my plans were not completely scuttled," snarled his uncle. "You presented the very glass and fashion of the arrogant townsman." Gilles gave Angela a look of approval. "You've convinced 'em that you're head over heels in love with the fool, and the wedding so soon will cause less of a furor because of that." He gave her a leering smile. "Have you decided that it's to your advantage to obey me, then?"

He walked over to her and deliberately took her slender arm in his hand, crushing it slowly.

The pain was intense, and Angela, lifting her beautiful gray eyes to meet his challenging stare, did not try to conceal her misery. "What use to rebel?" she asked weakly. "You are the master here."

It was what he wanted to hear, but his hard gaze continued to search her features. At length he released her arm. The agony of returning sensation almost caused her to cry out, but she smothered the sound. This final evidence of submission seemed to satisfy him.

When Poll had seen Angela into bed a short while later, the woman gave the girl a sly smile. "I'll be busy elsewhere tonight, Miss," she said. "I'll just lock you in."

Angela shrugged and turned away to hide

51

the excitement she feared might be visible on her face. "I'm sleepy," she murmured.

Angela waited for three hours before she made the move she had so carefully planned during the last two nights. Without lighting even one candle, she slipped into her clothing— the voluminous old weeds Marian had worn to Aunt Alys's funeral—and, retrieving her leather drawstring pouch from under the bed where she had hidden it, she crept to the door of her bedroom.

It had not been too difficult to pocket the butler's master key during the latter part of the evening. He had hung it on the hook in the pantry, as usual, before he went up to bed. As Angela knew, it fitted all the bedroom doors. Even as she turned it, the girl held her breath lest, even now, Gilles might have recollected that small fact and be hastening to prevent her escape. But the upper hallway was silent and empty; her stepfather was too drunk or too well occupied with Poll to concern himself about the girl he thought he had mastered completely.

Angela crept down the back stairs to the kitchen. It was still warm from the business of the day. As she eased open the back door, Angela sent one loving farewell thought to her mother and the home where they had been happy with Denzil Swann. Then, quietly closing the door, she made her way to the stables without a backward glance.

In the warm and redolent darkness of the stable, the girl began to saddle the gentle mare she always rode.

"What be ye about, Missie? Ye'll never want to be ridin' off at this hour?" came a voice at her shoulder.

Rigid with shock, Angela dared not even turn her head to see who had discovered her flight. Nausea rose in her throat at the disappointment—so close to escape! Then, past the barrier of shock, she recognized the voice. The speaker was Old Beamish! With no alternative, she threw herself upon the old fellow's mercy.

"I am running away from home, Beamish," she whispered. "I cannot stand to be near Mr. Loring."

The ancient servant shouldered past her and began to saddle the mare. "I'll lead 'er out to the trees for ye, Missie. Slip away now, lest the stableboy hears ye."

Thankfully Angela obeyed, but while she waited under the trees, all the consequences which might arise from her behavior came home to her. If anyone discovered Old Beamish in the act of helping her to escape from her home, the old fellow would have no hope of avoiding dismissal. Loring might even whip him first, to impress upon the rest of the staff the folly of disobedience. Even if Beamish could keep her name out of it, he would have to be sharper then she thought him to be, to find an excuse for saddling a horse at that time of night. Even supposing that he was not discovered at his task, and that she herself got safely away, how could Beamish explain the absence of Miss Angela's mare when he was supposed to keep night guard of the stable?

The girl was almost ready to run away without the mare when a better idea came into her head. Almost immediately, as upon cue, Old Beamish appeared beside her, holding Molly's reins.

"I will tell you what I am going to do, Beamish," she began in a very low voice. "I intend to drown at Spanish Cove, and you must discover Molly saddled outside the stable at dawn."

Even in the moonlight it was easy to read the alarm on the old man's face. "Now, now, Missie," he began, in the manner of one seeking to pacify a dangerous lunatic, "there must be a better way, surely? Parson Quayle could advise ye—"

"No, no, Beamish, I do not intend *actually* to drown myself! Merely to leave an extra set of clothing upon the beach at the Cove, so that whoever finds it will *assume* I have drowned! Do you not see, Beamish? If I am thought to have died, then Mr. Loring will not bother to search for me."

Old Beamish had many good qualities, but suffering fools gladly was not one of them. "If ever I heard such a knock-in-the-cradle! Your own father taught you to swim in the river, and you've paddled around in the Spanish Cove adunnamany times, to *my* certain knowledge! A sharp like Gilles Loring ain't goin' to be diddled by any such bookish notion! Drowned in Spanish Cove—what a totty-headed idea!" His rheumy old eyes glared at her in the moonlight. "I suppose ye know the gypsies are camped at the Cove? If ye think they'd let a prime mare like Molly come back to the stable, you're fair and far off! Nor they wouldn't leave a bundle o' good clothes sittin' on the sand, neither! So there'd be nothin' to tie you to the Cove. No, Missie, ye'd best just take Molly and go. I'll say I fell asleep."

Angela was about to give way to despair when an idea flashed into her mind. "Take off Molly's saddle, Beamish," she whispered urgently. "I'll remove the reins and bridle. I shall ride Molly to the crossroads and wave down the early stagecoach as it slows for the hill. As soon as I reach the crossroads, I'll turn Molly loose. She'll come back here. Can you wait up and return her to her stall?"

"Why not?" grumbled the old fellow. "Been puttin' 'em in an' takin' 'em out for ninety years."

Angela chuckled. "Thank you, Beamish," she breathed. She scrambled up onto Molly's back with a boost from the old groom, and taking the

55

mane firmly in her hands, guided the docile little mare through the trees to the road.

Within half an hour she had dismounted at the crossroads and sent Molly home with a sharp slap. Then the girl sat down on a milestone to await the coming of the London coach.

Chapter 5

ANGELA's escape was more easily accomplished than she had dared to hope. The coachman of the London stage had had to slow his tired team for the hill leading to the crossroads, and he was willing to take notice of the wildly waving arms of the small funereal figure which hailed him in the dawn. He did not carry complaisance so far as to dismount and open the door of the coach for her, but one of the passengers, a weedy youth, thrust the door open almost in her face, and gave her a hand up.

The coach was not too crowded, which might have accounted for the coachman's willingness to halt. Three of the five inside passengers were drowsing lethargically after the long, uncomfortable night. The weedy youth informed her that they were not to pause for breakfast for at least another hour. This naturally pleased the girl, now well embarked upon her desperate adventure. She peered shyly at her fellow passengers from under the short veil of her mother's black bonnet. An elderly couple dozed on the rear seat, the man's head on his wife's ample shoulder. Opposite them, a sour-faced man in neat professional black snored against the greasy upholstery.

Directly across from Angela lounged a colorful figure, a young woman in a red and white striped robe *à la Polonaise,* very low cut in front, over which she had draped a brown shawl. Her face, in the unflattering light of dawn, was revealed to be covered with a heavy layer of paint, and her bright yellow hair was topped by an elaborate hat, now askew. On her lap she held a black leather case, upon which she rested her forearms securely. Angela could hardly tear her startled gaze from this extraordinary vision.

The girl greeted her wondering stare with a frown. "You'll know me next time you see me," she sneered. "God save me from Quakers and country bumpkins! You're not just a fashion plate from *La Belle Assemblée* yourself, in that dismal getup," she went on. "Somebody died?"

Then, catching the sudden spasm of grief which crossed Angela's face, the other girl said less harshly. "I'm sorry! I guess I'm tired. It's been a long night!" and she cast a crabbed look at the other occupants of the coach. "Who was it then, love?"

"My mother was buried yesterday," Angela said quietly.

58

The other girl wasted little sympathy. "And now you're off to the great city to make your fortune?" teased the garishly dressed inquisitor; then, without waiting for a reply, she went on, "Goin' on the stage, are you?" She chuckled at her own jest. "Or have you got some relatives to give you a home? Mind they don't make a rotten drudge of you! That's what happened to me."

Angela's surprised look set her companion to giggling. "Bet you're thinkin' I don't much resemble a drudge." She preened her body in the gaudy robe. The weedy youth was watching her, wide-eyed.

"I soon caught on to what they planned for me," the girl continued. "I stayed just long enough to find my way about, and then I left 'em—with a very handsome gent who'd come to call on my cousin." She laughed. "Shouldn't think Maude's forgiven me yet! For all I care!"

Angela drew a deep breath. This young woman had lived! And in spite of all the cautionary tales, she seemed to be enjoying her life. Pushing back her own bonnet, which the jolting of the coach had tipped forward, she said, "I am Angela—" A horrid thought struck her. She could be traced by her name! "—Angela Smith. May I know your name?"

The other girl favored her with a pert grin. "Oh, I'm called Zalie. Like you, I have trouble remembering my last name." She giggled. "Well,

Angie, since we'll have to spend the devil of a time in this godawful bone-shaker of a coach, I'm glad we're going to be friends."

It was pleasant to talk to a bright, irreverent young woman like Zalie, Angela decided. For so long she had had no one of her own age, no cheerful young companion like this girl, who refused to be intimidated by the minatory looks of her fellow passengers or the encroaching advances of the weedy youth. When the coachman finally permitted a stop, Angela ate her breakfast with the best appetite she had had for weeks. She and Zalie shared a settle near the fire at the inn, and made short work of the fairly appetizing meal which was thrust at them by a harassed slavey. Angela noted that Zalie kept her black leather case on her lap throughout the meal, awkward though it proved to be. She herself kept the string of Marian's pouch firmly about her own wrist, so she quite understood Zalie's action. When a girl is alone in the world, she must cling to her belongings, no matter how few or how humble! She was moved to say as much to Zalie, and received a sharp glance in return. Perhaps it made the other girl feel less secure to know that she had betrayed her secret concern?

Bowling along in the coach once more after breakfast, Zalie continued to prove herself an amusing companion, and Angela even went so far as to ask her, in a voice below the hearing of their neighbors, if she knew of any situation Angela might secure in London.

The other girl raised a mocking eyebrow. "Sure you want to go to the Wicked City, love? You could stop at a smaller town, and find less to frighten you."

It was kindly meant, Angela knew, but she dared not disclose that she sought the anonymity of the great Metropolis in order to be safely hidden from her stepfather. So she made some offhand remark about wanting to see London, and turned the subject.

By dusk, both girls were feeling the strain of the endless jolting and swaying. They were hungry, too, and eager to leave the confines of the coach. As the carriage drew into the cobbled courtyard of a large posting house called Pride of Exeter, Zalie peered out of the small window and made a suggestion.

"Lots of folk stop overnight, Angie, and go on again in the morning when they're rested. Why don't we get a small room—oh, very cheap, for we haven't money to burn!—and lay up for the night?"

Angela's exhausted body clamored agreement, while her cautious mind was still trying to figure out how much it would cost and whether Gilles might be likely to trace her here. She gave way to her body's demands and got down from the coach as soon as the inn ostler swung the door open. First, however, she sought out the coachman and paid her fare, allowing him to think that this was her final destination. Then she went into the hostelry to seek Zalie. She found her new friend in the taproom, just finishing a small ale. Zalie was able to inform her that they could have the use of a room "under the eaves, but that's no matter; it'll be warmer there."

The cost was small enough to surprise Angela, who had not traveled recently, and when she had, not under such spartan circumstances. The girls proceeded at once into the Ordinary, where they had a satisfying meal of beef and cabbage and potatoes, all ladled from the same pot, for a reasonable sum. Angela found it delicious.

When they sat back, replete, Zalie grinned at her companion. "Don't need a chaperone when I've got you along, Angie! That rig-out is enough to scare off the bucks. Don't it put you in the dismals to wear such ugly duds?"

Angela considered the question seriously. She could hardly admit that she regarded the costume as a useful disguise, for her new friend would immediately wish to be told why a disguise was necessary. So she shook her head and smiled sleepily. "I'm so tired. Can we go to our room now, do you think?"

"Of course, if you want to," agreed Zalie. Then, with a glance around the rapidly filling Ordinary, she rose quickly. "Yes, let's go up."

As they walked toward the door, Angela's

glance was caught by the serious, wide blue gaze of a big man who had been facing them as they ate. He had a splendid, heavyset body and a craggy face crowned with sandy hair. Strangely, Angela found no menace in the steady scrutiny of those remarkable blue eyes. As she passed the man, she pulled down the veil of her bonnet to conceal her face from any further glances, however.

When they had clambered up the last of several staircases, the girls were too winded even to speak. Gasping, Zalie pushed open the door into the tiniest room Angela had ever seen. A single bed filled it almost from wall to wall. There was one tiny round window, up under the roof. There was neither chest of drawers, wardrobe, nor closet. Just a bed and four walls. Zalie stared around unbelievingly.

"Well, we won't get lost if we walk in our sleep," she commented finally.

Angela giggled. "There's nowhere to walk to," she agreed.

There was smothered laughter as they divested themselves of their outer garments, seated upon the bed as they did so. Zalie squeezed her square leather case under the bed and settled down above it, lounging against the headboard, obviously ready for a comfortable girlish coze. Angela was not so forthcoming, but she did enjoy the other girl's spirited comments upon their fellow-travelers, the meals they had been served, and the hazards of life in a big city. Just as Angela's eyelids were beginning to droop over her eyes, Zalie startled her with a sudden request.

"Angie, can I tell you something important?"

"Yes, of course, Zalie. If you wish to."

"I am running away from a horrid marriage."

Angela sat upright in the bed, eyes and mouth open.

"No!"

"Yes," said Zalie, with considerable satisfaction. Her eyes were intent upon the open, unguarded countenance beside her. "It is almost like a play upon the stage." This was not really so remarkable, since it was from that exact source that Zalie had filched the idea. "My wicked uncle wishes me to marry a man of his choice, and I hate the creature! So I am running away!"

Angela was betrayed by this amazing coincidence into a reckless disclosure. "But that is my own case exactly! I am running away from a repugnant marriage also!"

"So that's the reason for your somber disguise," mused Zalie. Then she smiled pityingly. "My dear girl, you only make yourself unforgettable in that rig! If your father has ever caught sight of that costume, he will have no trouble identifying you—and it!—at first glimpse!"

Angela was forced to admit that Zalie's comment made sense. And Gilles had seen the clothing, had even lifted it in disparaging hands.

Still, he had never actually seen her in it. She shook her head. Meeting Zalie's bright curious glance she said slowly, "I shall have to take my chances. I have no other clothing."

Zalie clapped her hands with a loud laugh. "But *I have!* And I've just conceived the perfect scheme. We'll change clothes!"

Angela frowned. "Change?"

Zalie indicated her red and white striped polonaise, casually tossed over the foot of the bed. "You wear that and I'll sport your gloomy draperies. Then if your father or my uncle catch up with us, they'll pick up the wrong girl and give the other one a fine chance to escape!"

For a minute Angela was tempted. Surely Gilles, searching for his drab little stepchild, would never give a second glance to the wearer of that garish costume. Then the thought of Gilles, or anyone else, seeing her with her bosom so exposed was too disturbing to contemplate. She shook her head.

"It wouldn't fadge. My—figure is not as full as yours. I couldn't hold it up."

"We could pin it," Zalie persisted.

Angela said more positively, "No, Zalie. You know how you'd hate to be seen in my dismal rig-out. You said so yourself." She softened the refusal with a smile as she pulled the counterpane over her.

Shrugging, Zalie blew out the candle.

*   *   *

Angela awoke the next morning to an unaccustomed racket. Eyes closed, she tried to sort out and identify the sounds: the shouts of men, the rattle of horses' hooves on cobbles, the crunch and screech of carriage wheels, the slamming of doors. . . . She stretched and opened her eyes, reassured by this loud evidence of her escape from peaceful Swanholme.

The first sight which caught her attention was the gaudy red and white polonaise draped causally at the foot of the bed. Turning to smile at her companion, Angela was surprised to find the space empty. She sat up abruptly. Zalie would hardly have left their tiny room without first donning her dress—yet there was no place within that tiny cell where she could be hiding. Angela's eyes widened. One more fact suddenly thrust itself into her mind. Her own clothing, neatly folded over the footboard the previous evening, was nowhere to be seen! Scrambling down the bed, the girl peered over the footboard. No heap of dark cloth met her frantic gaze. The incredible idea had to be accepted. Somehow, stealthily and silently during the night, Zalie had dressed in Angela's clothing and left the room.

But why would a girl play such a trick, exchanging her own garments for a costume she had derided? Angela caught her breath. Exchange! The last thing Zalie had talked about as they were preparing to go to sleep was her preposterous proposal that the girls change clothing! But Angela had rejected the idea.

It now appeared that Zalie had not.

Angela was appalled. On the first day of her escape to freedom she had already lost her clothes, the concealing, black-veiled bonnet and the cloak which had given her anonymity and a measure of respect. This gaudy costume of Zalie's would make her the cynosure of all eyes. No one could avoid glancing at the garish thing! Its wearer would be hard to forget!

"I might as well carry a placard," fumed Angela, sick at heart. Then a more devastating thought struck her. Marian's leather pouch! Had Zalie taken that also?

Scrambling back to her pillow, Angela searched frantically underneath it, then closed on a comforting shape. At least Zalie had confined her theft to an unsanctioned exchange of garments. Angela crouched down and peered under the bed. Zalie's leather case was gone.

Grimly the girl dressed in the polonaise, considered and rejected with a shudder the beplumed and flowered bonnet, and, after combing her long, lustrous black hair and braiding it in a thick coronet, draped Zalie's heavy woolen shawl over her head and crossed the ends decently over her exposed bosom. There was no mirror, but Angela knew she had done her possible to present a decorous front to the world.

Hurrying down the flights of stairs, she found her hostess caught up in the breakfast bustle of her kitchen. It was some reassurance to learn that Zalie had paid her own share of the night's lodging.

"She has gone without speaking to me," the girl explained her query.

"Oh, well, she's paid, Miss." The landlord's wife's brief glance at the red and white striped dress indicated her opinion of it. "Poor widow lady, she had other things on her mind, I'll be bound!"

"But she isn't—" began Angela, and then closed her lips firmly. What was done was done. "Do you remember when she left?"

"She was in the kitchen at first light," answered the good woman, a little restive at this inquisition. "Now if you'll just excuse me, Miss—"

"Did she mention her destination?" persisted Angela. If it was London, it might be possible to trace Zalie and get Marian's mourning clothes back.

"She said she was going north to Scotland," vouchsafed the landlord's wife. "Took the early stagecoach north, I remember. Quite a rush to get her on it before it left."

So Zalie had at least begun the journey north. Angela had no confidence that Scotland was the girl's real destination, and she had no money to pursue a wild-goose chase. Sighing, Angela permitted herself to be directed to the Ordinary to break her fast.

"You've plenty of time, Miss, before the next coach comes through for London," the landlord's wife informed her.

In spite of the tasty breakfast, Angela's mood was glum. To the anticipated charges on her slender store of money she would now have to add a sum large enough to purchase a more suitable costume. At length, clasping her leather pouch close to her, Angela went out into the courtyard and prepared to wait for permission to board the stagecoach for London, which had just pulled in and was having fresh horses put to.

The vehicle was standing near the high-arched entrance, its coachman and guard in impassioned discussion with the inn's head groom. The argument, easily overheard by virtue of the loudness of the participants' voices, was apparently based on the coachman's disgust at the team the ostlers had figged out for him.

"—naught but a bloody set o' plough horses, Grum!" he was shouting.

"Oh, yers?" riposted the groom. "An' I s'pose you was expectin' a turnout of sixteen-mile-an-hour tits?" He jeered. "Get on yer way, Tommy Onslow!"

Muttering malediction, the coachman strode over to mount his box. The guard followed quickly, and a straggle of passengers hastened out to join those already in the coach, lest it should take off without them. Angela was hurriedly bringing up in the rear when a sudden commotion drew all eyes.

Into the courtyard galloped a splendid pair, foam-flecked, wild-eyed, pulling a natty curricle on the seat of which sat two gentlemen dressed in a very dashing style. As they sighted the London coach, they gave tongue vociferously.

"Stop! Hold the coach!"

The coachman was heard to express his distaste for flash coves who had no more sense than to disrupt the schedules of honest drivers. However, since the curricle was barring his way, the said honest driver could do nothing but pause to allow the dilatory creatures to join the party.

It appeared, however, that to join the passengers on their trip to London was not the purpose of either of the men in the curricle. While the stockier of the two held the horses, his companion leaped down and ran toward the coach. Everyone present was startled to hear him cry, in tones of unmistakable triumph, "Zalie! So I have caught you! *Stop, thief!*"

Saying which, the newcomer seized the stunned Angela by one shoulder and whirled her to face him. "Where are they, you cheap little slut? What have you done with the jewels?" And he shook her so hard the brown shawl fell from her head.

The guard and coachman stared down with rising suspicion at Angela. Passengers craned avidly from the narrow windows to enjoy the sensational doings. Numbers of persons who had no connection with the affair came hastening from all directions to discover the cause of the uproar. Quaking with alarm, Angela faced her accuser wide-eyed.

She saw a handsome, rather dissolute, and at the moment, very angry countenance, marked by heavy black eyebrows, dark eyes, and a full red mouth. At the moment the eyebrows were lifted in astonishment.

"You're not Zalie!" cried the angry man. "But you're wearing the dress she coaxed me to buy her just three days ago—the little thief!"

· Angela found her voice in this extreme emergency. "Your precious Zalie has just robbed me of my own garments and left me to wear these—*things,"* she began, but her accuser was having none of such implausible excuses.

"You're in league with the bitch to chouse me! I know your kind! You've changed clothes to confuse pursuit, but you will be meeting her somewhere to cut up the loot, I'll swear!" He shook Angela until her shawl slipped from its precarious drape over her shoulders and pulled away from her breast. Momentarily caught by the sight of such tender adolescent charms in a garment made for a more buxom figure, the accuser grinned involuntarily. "Didn't have time to patch it up? I'd like to see Zalie in a dress that fitted *you!* A regular bodice-buster, Zalie is!"

At this point the landlord came bustling up, and demanded to know by what right the gentlemen dared to halt the departure of a licensed stagecoach. The accuser, still gripping Angela tightly by the shoulder, turned to explain his action.

"This little ladybird has robbed me of a fortune, and I have just caught up with her. Unless she hands my jewels back to me at once, I shall call the constable! I am Lord Merrel, and my friend, Sir Horace Tilling, will vouch for my *bona fides.*"

"The gentleman is mistaken," protested Angela, but no one paid any attention to her. Instead, the landlord tore her leather pouch from her grasp and thrust it at her accuser.

"Take it, and let the stage go," he ordered.

Since Lord Merrel was standing with his back to the open door, the coach could not move without knocking him down.

"Not until I make sure Zalie isn't hiding inside," stated his lordship. "Hold this one while I look."

The landlord took Angela by the arm, and Sir Horace, consigning his winded team to an ostler, ran over to join the fun. He took Angela's other arm, stared at her, and said, "But this ain't Zalie!" in tones of simple surprise.

"I told you I was not!" cried Angela, but again no one listened to her.

Milord climbed down out of the coach with great dissatisfaction. "We must get to the bottom of this," he announced, and pulled Angela away from the landlord's grip. Just as the latter was about to slam the door of the coach, a passenger disembarked and stood quietly observing the scene as the coach rolled away through the archway, its occupants craning for a last look at the tableau in the courtyard. One pair of eyes was startled, angry, unbelieving.

Angela, trying to hold the gaping bodice closed with one hand, was leaning down to pick up her shawl with the other. Lord Merrel pulled her upright and closer to him.

"What new tricks are you playing off?" he demanded. "You will come into the inn with me and be thoroughly examined at once! I'll find my jewels if I have to tear every shred of clothing from your body!"

The landlord did not seem to object to this method of examination, and Sir Horace seemed positively to welcome the idea, but one voice rose unexpectedly in Angela's defense.

"It will be quite unnecessary to proceed to such extremes," said the man who had descended from the coach at the last minute. Angela's terrified gaze flew to his face. It was the big, sandy-haired traveler she had seen in the Ordinary the night before.

"And what business is this of yours?" demanded Lord Merrel.

"You might call it simple justice," answered the big man quietly. "This lady is not the one who was wearing that rather memorable costume last night when the coach arrived."

"What has that to say to anything?" sneered Lord Merrel. "The doxy changed with her confederate to confuse pursuit. I'll be bound Zalie's off somewhere with my jewels, and left this poor creature to take the blame. That's it!" he exclaimed, charmed with his own explanation. "Your confederate has duped you, little trull. Best tell us all you know. If you refuse, I'll hand you over to the constables at once. Grand Larceny is a hanging offense."

"Let us go inside," urged the sandy-haired man, advancing firmly upon Lord Merrel so that the latter was forced to move in the desired direction or be pushed aside. While his lordship obviously did not relish this sort of persuasion, the big quiet man offered so little excuse for belligerence that it seemed easier to conform than to argue. Thus the little procession made its way to the inn, the landlord thankfully leading it to a small private parlor.

Lord Merrel, retaining his grip upon Angela's arm, followed closely, while the sandy-haired man and Sir Horace brought up the rear. When he had them safely in the private parlor, the landlord, relieved to have this public scandal contained in decent privacy, asked one question.

"Does your lordship wish to summon Constable Littlefield?"

"Yes," said Lord Merrel.

"No," said the sandy-haired man.

"Who the devil are you?" snapped Lord Merrel, "and by what right are you interfering in what is none of your affair?"

"I am Richard Bennet of Bennet Farm, near Elsinghurst," said the big man. His quiet authority and huge, sturdy presence seemed to impress the landlord of the Pride of Exeter as much as did his well-cut coat and really superb boots. Not so the two noblemen.

"Oh, a farmer," sneered Sir Horace.

"Run along and harvest your crops," advised Lord Merrel.

The landlord stared at the speakers with dislike. "I have heard of Bennet Farm," he stated, "but I have not heard of a Merrel or a Tilling until this moment."

"Lord Elsingham of Elsingham Manor will stand warrant for me," said Richard Bennet quietly. "I was on the way to London on business of his when I arrived here last night."

That seemed to settle the matter for the landlord. "Do you vouch for this lady, Mr. Bennet?" he asked.

Richard Bennet looked deeper into the pleading gray eyes. "I do," he said quietly.

The landlord went out and closed the door. Let the Quality and the County Squire settle the matter between them, he thought. I have an Inn to run!

Chapter 6

RICHARD Bennet took the wind out of Lord Merrel's sails very neatly. Before the other man could open his mouth to launch a verbal attack, Richard deftly removed Angela from his loosened grip scorted her to a seat, and handed her her shawl. With a small tilt of his head and the ghost of a smile which was not visible to Lord Merrel or Sir Horace, he said gently, "This has been a shocking experience for you, my child. First robbed of your clothing, then mistaken for a thief! When the matter is made clear, I have no doubt Lord Merrel will make you a handsome apology—"

But this was going too far for the irascible nobleman.

"Apologize to that—" he began angrily. Then encountering Bennet's steely blue glance, he moderated the term he had intended to use, "—to that lady for her part in robbing me? You must be mad!"

"But you have not proven that the child had anything to do with robbing you, have you? So first we had better see whether the young lady has anything of yours in her reticule."

He took the drawstring pouch from Lord Merrel's surprised grasp and opened it, upending it gently on the table. The tiny child's ring, the miniature, the few coins tumbled out, well padded by Angela's simple underclothing and neat fichus and handkerchieves. While the men scrutinized the pitiful possessions, Richard picked up the ring in gentle fingers.

"Is this your jewelry, Milord?"

"Of course not! That trumpery bauble!" He eyed the white-faced girl. "But perhaps, somewhere on her person, she has them concealed. I shall investigate—if you gentlemen will leave us? Just to spare the chit's blushes, of course!" He grinned widely.

Sir Horace guffawed, and was understood to say that it was too bad of Julian to spoil sport. Richard Bennet did not seem to be amused. He put Angela's belongings carefully back in her pouch, closed it, and handed it to her. Then he addressed Lord Merrel in a rallying tone.

"You will do as you think wisest, of course. It seems to me that a man of your worldly knowledge, Milord, must be aware that no woman of the class you claim her to be would allow herself to be seen in a garment which looks like—*that.*"

Three pairs of masculine eyes, holding vastly different expressions, turned as one to stare at the baggy garment on the slight, girlish figure.

Lord Merrel grinned reluctantly. "Certainly Zalie wouldn't be caught dead in any costume which displayed her to such a disadvantage," he admitted. "But perhaps they had no time to do better."

"Why?" asked Richard quietly.

"Why?" the question seemed to surprise Lord Merrel.

"If this was a conspiracy, as you claim, why were the conspirators so ill prepared for their exchange of clothing?"

"The scheme was probably hatched last night, when the two women shared a room," suggested Sir Horace.

"Even then they would have done something to insure that the garments fitted. If your— friend's clothing looks so oddly upon this child, how must the child's garments look upon your friend?"

Julian laughed aloud at the image this conjured up. Diverted momentarily, he asked Angela, "How did she squeeze herself into your dress, girl?"

"I do not know, Milord," Angela admitted. "When I woke this morning Zalie was gone and my clothing with her. Also her black leather box."

"My jewels!" shouted Lord Merrel. "You *saw* them?"

"I saw only the box, and how carefully she kept it by her," Angela informed him. "But when I dressed in these garments she had left me, and went down to inquire of the landlord's wife as to Zalie's whereabouts, the woman told me she had taken the early stagecoach north to Scotland this morning." The girl faced the incredulity in Lord Merrel's expression. "I, too, Milord, took leave to doubt that Scotland was Zalie's real destination, but if you wish to find her, it should not be hard if you go at once, and follow the northbound coach. You might come up with it before it makes a posting stop, and Zalie has a chance to change either the coach or her clothes again. She is now wearing the most unfashionable garments of heavy black wool— my mother's mourning clothes. There is a black dress, a heavy black cloak, and a black bonnet with a face veil."

Sir Horace laughed heartily. "Can you picture Zalie in such a rig?" he asked. "She'll hate every minute she has to wear it!"

"I have no fear she'll soon chouse some other poor devil out of a new outfit! But I cannot accept that this little—lady knew nothing about the business," he added, his eyes searching out the details of Angela's slight figure and small, lovely face rather greedily. "Tell me something about yourself, my dear," he demanded. "If you

80

are not an accomplice of Zalie's, the disclosure of your own name and direction will exonerate you, will it not?"

Almost placidly Richard Bennet intervened. "Should you not rather be pursuing the elusive Zalie? If she has your family jewels, as you claim, she should surely not be permitted to escape to Scotland or anywhere else with them? I understand she has only a few hours start on you? The stage is a lumbering vehicle. Could it not be overtaken by a man with some skill at the reins?"

"He's right, you know, Julian," agreed Sir Horace enthusiastically. "Just time for a quencher and then on our way, eh? Tallyho!"

Lord Merrel elected to turn stubborn. "This *lady*," the emphasis was insulting, "has not yet seen fit to divulge her name and direction. I think it only common sense to make sure of so much, at least, before letting her go. I am not at all convinced she knows nothing more about the matter than she has admitted."

"I have given you my name and direction, sir," said Richard crisply. "I shall even write it down for you, if you feel you may have trouble remembering it."

"You go surety for this lady?" sneered Lord Merrel, plainly displeased at the farmer's intervention in what might otherwise have proved an easy conquest.

"I do," replied Richard quietly, warning signs

flying in his bright blue eyes. "Do you wish to dispute the matter?"

Sir Horace caught his friend's arm. "Not at all the thing, Julian, embroiling yourself in a meeting with a farmer over a little light-skirt! If your mamma came to hear of it—Besides, the farmer's in the right of it. Much better be off after the thief. She can't have gone far. We might even catch the coach before she can leave it!"

Whether this appeal to common sense, the threat of his mother's displeasure, or the hard gleam in Richard's eye had the most effect upon Lord Merrel would be hard to determine. In the event, his lordship allowed himself to be persuaded, and after accepting a slip from Bennet's notebook upon which that gentleman had inscribed his name and direction, and casting a long, probing glance at Angela, the nobleman quitted the inn with his friend.

Richard sat down in a chair across from Angela, and, grinning, heaved an exaggerated sigh of relief. "I feared that hothead might have called me out," he said, mendaciously. "My grandfather's blunderbuss is really too old to be counted on for accuracy."

Angela, who felt, at this moment of unexpected relief, more like weeping than laughing, found herself coaxed into a smile. Her new friend greeted this response with obvious relief. Getting up, he rang the bell for service. When the harried maidservant came to inquire as to his worship's needs, Richard ordered two cups of tea and some bicuits.

Grateful for this prosaic remedy, Angela pulled together her shattered wits and began to thank her rescuer. "For I cannot see how I could have convinced the gentlemen of my innocence, since I dared not tell them my name—" she began, and then caught herself short in dismay. *"Oh!"*

"Och, aye, I kenned as much," her new friend reassured her, dropping into a soft Scots accent which charmed the girl. " 'Twas for that very reason I led them off the scent with a wee bit of bluster and indirection." His bright blue eyes regarded her with flattering admiration. "Forbye, ye've no need to tell me one word more than you wish, although I confess I'm in hopes you may permit me to help you. For one thing," he added, before she could voice any objections, "you really must be rid of—er—Zalie's dress before you face the world."

Struck by the wisdom of this suggestion, Angela stared at the big man in gratitude. "I have not yet thanked you for getting back my bag for me," she said shyly. "As you know, having seen the contents, I am not well-to-pass. Still, you are correct in saying that I must not be seen in this—this *garment!* But how—"

"Will you not leave it to me, Miss—Och! I as good as said I would not press for your name, did I not? And here I am havering on about it.

Then how shall I address you? May I name you Miss Terry—because you present such a charming mystery to me?" he explained with a chuckle.

Angela found his gentle teasing so pleasant that she smiled quite spontaneously. At the enchanting sweetness of the expression Richard's eyes widened and then narrowed with interest. The girl was holding out her small hand, saying, "I am Angela Swann, of Swanholme near Averly in Cornwall. I am running away from my stepfather who planned to marry me to his nephew."

Richard's eyebrows did not rise, nor did he show any shock or alarm at this startlingly indecorous disclosure. "Did your mother agree to the marriage?" he asked gently.

"She died three days ago," Angela said forlornly. "My stepfather had arranged my marriage to take place—why, it was to be *today!*"

Richard smiled at her change of expression. "It would seem to be a blessed relief that you escaped the fellow," he congratulated her, pleased to have her mind off her sorrow. He continued briskly, "Let us see if we cannot contrive a more suitable costume, Miss Swann, for I greatly fear you will draw too much attention in that—ah—exotic plumage."

At this euphemistic description of the wretched dress, Angela actually laughed aloud. What a delightful Scottish gentleman this was, with his noble appearance and his droll wit! "You make the impossible appear easy," she said warmly. "How do you plan to achieve this miracle? I have just over three pounds—"

Richard wasted no time. Before the girl quite knew what was happening, he had arranged that the parlor be kept for Miss Terry's exclusive use; had somehow avoided taking the money she was trying to thrust upon him, and had sallied forth into the town to secure less conspicuous clothing for his charge. Angela sat in blessed privacy sipping the fragrant tea and nibbling biscuits hungrily, not trying too hard to puzzle out the reasons for her new friend's amazing kindness.

Within a remarkably short space of time, considering the results, Richard Bennet was back with a large, neatly wrapped parcel in his arms. This he deposited in Angela's arms, brushed off her timid thanks, and disappeared while she donned the new dress. Angela made haste to unwrap the bundle. Her eyes widened at the dove gray dress revealed. It was exactly the color of her eyes—had he noticed—and was of the type called "riding coat," or, in the vernacular, "redingote," with revers and a triple falling collar. Angela, smoothing the gray superfine over her gently rounded hips, was lost in admiration of the elegant garment. Timidly she opened the door, to find her champion standing guard in the corridor. He entered the parlor at her invitation, hands held behind him, and proceeded to give the new costume an admiring survey. He seemed to find it more than adequate.

"I am informed," he stated with a twinkle deep in his blue eyes, "that this dress is 'all the crack,' whatever that means!"

"It is *le dernier cri*," Angela sighed blissfully. "You were not misinformed, sir."

"I'll admit 'tis a braw jupe, lassie, and you're as comely as a young wood violet in it."

Angela felt herself blushing. No man had ever paid her such a charming compliment, and while she wasn't too sure of the meaning of 'braw jupe,' the look in Richard Bennet's eyes told her it must be high praise in Scotland.

He brought his hand around from behind his back and held out a small hatbox. "Just for purposes of disguise, solely," he said airily, fending off her embarrassed gratitude.

What a good man he is! the girl thought. Then she saw the hat, and words left her. It was an inspired creation of massed, tiny, silk-velvet violets, with a chiffon veil in the same color down to the chin. Angela neither knew nor cared if it was suitable to wear with the redingote, but fell instantly in love with it.

Richard was scrutinizing her intently. He stepped forward and lifted his hands to her head. Angela stopped breathing. Gently the man adjusted the frivolous trifle upon the shining dark hair; stood back, frowning fiercely, then nodded with a smile of satisfaction.

"Perfect!" announced Richard Bennet.

Angela allowed herself to breathe again. Then, minding her manners, she tried to thank Richard for his kindness, his generosity, his expert taste and knowledge. This gave her pause.

"How *did* you know, Richard? My size, I mean. For this lovely redingote fits as though it had been tailored for me—"

"Now that *was* a bit of skill on my part," acknowledged her benefactor cheerfully. "I told the good lady that you were as slender and graceful as a young willow, beautiful as a wood violet, and just as high as my heart—and you see I was exactly right!"

Dissolved in a gust of irresistible laughter, Angela felt her fears draining away, and in their place, a sort of delightful warmth she had never before experienced. "Oh, Richard!" she said softly. "It is the most beautiful hat I have ever seen! And the redingote so elegant! Thank you! Now you must tell me the cost, if you please!" She was resolved to keep them if she had to make payments to her benefactor for the next ten years.

But somehow in the next few hurried minutes, the subject of repayment seemed to get lost, as Richard, very brisk and businesslike, advised sternly, "We must make haste, now, lest your stepfather is on his way to search for you, and should find us here! I have hired us a gig, if you will not mind riding in an open carriage in all your finery? There are some pleasant shortcuts I know of, which will keep us far from the highway along which you might be expected to be found!"

Quite swept away by Richard's urgency, Angela kept enough of her wits about her to ask, albeit diffidently, where they were bound? To which her protector, staring at her in a bemused way for a moment, replied that they would go at once to his sister, Miss Margaret Bennet, "For you will be aware," he said with a pawky Scots complacence, "that you must have a chaperone as soon as possible!"

Forced to acknowledge the wisdom of this decision, Angela recollected an earlier remark by the same gentleman. "But did I not understand you to say you were on your way to London on a commission for Lord Elsingham?"

"I believe I have changed my mind," said Richard. "I forgot something I shall be needing in the near future, and have decided to go home for it first, before proceeding to the Metropolis." Then, meeting her sceptical glance, he went on broadly, "Ah'm not usually sae shatter-brained, ye ken, so ye see 'twas a maircy Ah encountered ye in the coachyard!"

Angela stared fascinated at her new friend's tanned cheeks and observed the color rising in them. Richard was blushing! It was clear that he was going out of his way to get her bestowed in some safe place. Her innocent heart softened with gratitude. She did not argue further with him, preferring to accept his courtesy in the spirit in which it was offered. *He is a true knight,* she told herself, *and I am the damsel in distress he is rescuing! I must be worthy of his great kindness. Perhaps his sister will let me work for her about the farm. Or she may know of employment I can get, and be able to repay some small part of my debt to Richard.* Lost in these plans, Angela allowed herself to be shepherded into a smart little gig, her pouch handed to her, and a light robe draped across the elegant gray dress. Then Richard mounted beside her, thanked the grinning host with a smile and a word, and tooled the gig smartly out through the archway, across the highroad, and into a delightfully green country lane.

Chapter 7

IT was almost dusk when Richard turned the gig in between neatly-painted white posts flanking a wide lane, deep-set between high, hedged banks.

"The Farm is just a mile now," he assured her. "It is my sincere hope that the long drive has not tired you too much."

Angela shook her head. "How could it? You have taken every care for my comfort—dinner at that dear little inn, frequent stops to view a pretty pastoral scene! And this gig is much more comfortable than the coach. I was sure I had not an unbroken bone in my body last night!"

Richard laughed, a deep sound which rumbled in his massive chest. He had enjoyed the day more than he could recall doing for a long time. Then it struck him like a blow that he had not once, until this moment, remembered his lost love. It was a memory which had haunted him daily for nearly five years. *Kathryn!* He waited for the familiar rush of pain.

It did not come.

Richard frowned. It was not like him to forget the woman he had loved and lost. He stared ahead with a somber visage, mentally castigating himself for a faithless clod. The girl beside him wondered, with a little clutch of fear, what she had said or done to bring so forbidding an expression to her companion's handsome countenance. Too shy and too newly his friend to ask, she set her own lips against further chattering. She began to worry, for the first time during the drive, about her situation, and her chances of securing the much needed work.

The man became conscious of the new rigidity of her attitude. Poor little thing, he thought, she is quite foredone with all the excitements and worries of the day! Compassion sent his own dark memories into hiding. "Are ye weary, poor little lass?" he queried gently. "My sister Margaret will have a warm welcome for ye, I promise."

The enormity of her presumption overwhelmed the girl. "I am imposing! I cannot think how I could have agreed to this!" she wailed softly. "I should never have come with you! Tomorrow I must find employment somewhere, so that I may keep myself, and not be a burden upon—upon strangers!" Her great tear-filled eyes were lifted to his, her small face desolate. "What must you think of me, Richard Bennet!"

Richard's sandy eyebrows drew across his strong nose in a self-condemning frown. "Now whatever have I done to put ye in such a fret?" he asked. "How could a little one like you be a burden? Can ye no' accept that my sister and I are eager to be your friends? There is time and to spare for finding work, bairn. When ye're ready, Maggie will be pleased to help ye!" As he talked soothingly, he was relieved to see her tense, strained little face soften into calmness, and the haunted light go out of her eyes.

Angela stared toward the farmhouse they were now approaching. She must not let this wonderful man see how much she admired him, lest she create a problem for him and his sister with her unwanted affection. The wisest course would be to maintain a calm air of polite interest in the farm, and arrange to get herself out of their lives as quickly as possible. Unfortunately at this moment she recalled one of Gilles Loring's inelegant maxims: "Fish and guests stink after three days." But even Gilles had allowed for three days of hospitality! Angela promised herself she would be out of the Bennets' lives within the prescribed time.

She forced her attention back to her host. Richard was pointing out with obvious pride the special beauties of his noble holding. The place surprised her, being larger than any farm she had seen near Averly. The buildings were better kept than even those at Swanholme. There were wide paddocks, white-fenced; sturdy barns and stables; three small cottages, each within its circle of flowering shrubs and trees. These cottages, Richard explained, were the homes of his married farm workers and their young families. All was orderly, peaceful, richly productive. Angela eyed Richard with renewed respect. As he brought the gig to a halt, she smiled up at him with her heart in her innocent face. Richard bent over and kissed her gently on the lips.

Observing this tableau with startled interest, a sweet-faced little woman stood on the front porch smiling a cheerful welcome.

"Back so soon, Richard? That must surely be the quickest trip to London ever made!" From her smile, it was plain that Maggie Bennet knew he had not completed his journey, and shrewdly guessed at his reason for so speedy a return, for her next words were a warm greeting to the girl who was blushing and smiling almost apprehensively at her.

"Come away in, my dear," she said cordially. "I've just put the tea to steep, and the scones are hot from the oven."

"Och, you were expecting us, then!" teased Richard. "And here we were thinkin' we'd be givin' ye a fine surprise!" He helped the girl down from the gig and handed the reins to a

94

tall, grinning lad who'd appeared from behind the house. "Maggie, this is our new friend Angela Swann. I've brought her to stay with us for a wee while. She has just lost her dear mother, and had a bit of trouble with a very wicked stepfather—just like in the fairy tales. Angela, this is my sister Margaret."

Miss Bennet beamed a welcome and pulled the girl gently toward the house. "I'll just show you your room, Angela, and when you have freshened up from your long drive, come to the kitchen and we'll all have a cup of tea."

Suiting action to word, the woman led Angela to a delightful little room on the upper floor and pointed out the rose-painted basin and the ewer filled with fresh water, and the little china dish holding homemade lavender soap. At the sight and scent of this commodity, which had always been a pleasant product of Marian Swann's housewifery also, sudden tears flooded the girl's eyes. She put her hands up to her face in a gesture of desolation.

Instantly two warm arms were close about her shoulders, and a gentle voice which echoed Richard's Scotts burr was offering comfort and condolence.

"There, there, now, lassie! Can you tell Maggie what's the matter?"

To deny such loving-kindness was beyond the girl. Angela recounted the story of the last few terrible days, omitting nothing. It was a blessed relief to share it all—her grief for her mother, her fear of Loring's cruelty, her distaste for the foppish Vivian, her frightening realization that she had no one to turn to in her own home, her revulsion against her stepfather.

"Gilles has always beaten me and my mother, but that last day, Miss Bennet, he looked at me so queerly . . . when he spoke about—about younger, fresher bodies . . ." Angela put her hands to her face again. "Oh, ma'am, I had the most . . . the most fearful notion that he . . . meant me!" she whispered.

Maggie Bennet's face was a study in concern for the child, and anger and disgust at the stepfather. All she said, as she patted the girl's slender shoulder, was a quiet, "You are safe here, child. We shall not let that monster harm you."

Brave words, she thought to herself as she held the trembling girl and murmured words of comfort. Brave words, but what could we do if the brute presented himself and demanded the custody of his own stepdaughter? Richard would make a good fight of it, that went without saying. She knew his strength, and his ready compassion for the underdog, but how far could his integrity prevail against the force of the law? Smothering a sigh, she put the girl gently from her and offered a smile.

"Take off that pretty bonnet, child, comb your hair, and wash your face and hands. Then I'll show you to the kitchen. It's the heart of Bennet Farm, Miss Swann—"

"Oh, please, could you call me Angela?" begged the girl.

"Angela," agreed Maggie indulgently.

The girl smiled with such sweetness that Maggie felt a pleasant stir of surprise. A wild idea flashed through her sisterly mind. As she watched the child reverently deposit the concoction of violets and net upon the lowboy—had *Richard* actually picked that out, as the girl averred?—the wild idea took root and began a tentative growth. The clothing, so very stylish and appropriate: wherever had Richard acquired the *nous* to select such items of a woman's wardrobe? And there was that gentle kiss of welcome at the front door! Had Richard decided he had grieved long enough over his hopeless, unspoken love for the lovely Lady Elsingham? As Angela brushed her long, lustrous black hair and tidied her slender person in the new gray costume which exactly matched her dove-gray eyes, Maggie made a resolve. Richard was too much a man to be wasted upon a doomed dream! The older woman nodded her head decisively and led the girl down to the kitchen There they found the man waiting with such a look of interest and pleasure on his face as Maggie had not seen for too many years.

Chapter 8

ANGELA spent the next week in a daze of happiness. Somehow she was not able to insist upon seeking employment in the district, for every time she broached the subject, either Maggie Bennet or Richard had some pressing project for which they needed her immediate help. Maggie disclosed an urgent need to rearrange the storage closets. She and Angela spent a busy, exhausting, but very satisfying day in the pantry, lifting every one of dozens of pots of jam and jelly and pickles from their shelves, washing the shelves, washing and checking the pots, restoring vanished labels, and reshelving the bounteous stores.

Another day the girl was recruited to assist in the churning of butter, although to her knowledge there were two milkmaids and the buxom young wife of one of the herdsmen who assisted in the dairy and kitchen when required. No matter! Angela loved every minute of the bright, cheerful days and the peaceful, flower-scented nights.

One day near the end of the week, when he had returned from the postponed trip to London, Richard confided in the girl that he thought his sister was too housebound, and suggested that Angela coax her to make an expedition to the picturesque ruins of an ancient monastery by a lake.

"We'll take a basket o' goodies wi' us, plenty o' san'wiches an' cake, an' we can boil up billikin for tea when we're thirsty," he wheedled with a brazen exaggeration of his usual faint Scottish accent. "Puir Maggie's lookin' wan an' weary. 'Twould be no more than simple Christian charity to get the poor housebound woman out for a bit!" Since this last phrase sounded, in Richard's deep voice, like "puir hoose-booned wummun oot," Angela could not help giggling. Richard's elated grin warned her that he was quite aware of the effect he was having on her, and shamelessly gloried in it. She tried to harden her heart against the Scotsman's charm, but it was useless. Angela was forced to admit, also, that she owed the Bennets more than she could ever pay. It was no more than just, she convinced herself, to try her hand at persuading Maggie.

"You can begin this very minute," the big fellow advised her, "for here is Herself as if on cue!"

Maggie regarded the conspirators with an indulgent smile.

"Whatever are ye up to, ye rapscallions? 'Tis plain there's a muckle more brewin' than a pot o' tea!"

Angela, whose life had been singularly free of teasing jokes and easy camaraderie, bloomed in the warmth of this delightful atmosphere. She even ventured a mild jest of her own. "I wonder why it is," she said with a shy sparkle in her beautiful gray eyes, "that the Bennet family suddenly displays a pronounced Scots burr when it's up to mischief?"

Her auditors chuckled and exchanged glances.

"Caught in the act," confessed Richard. "I was coaxing Angela to take a picnic to the ruined abbey with us."

"An excellent idea!" said Maggie instantly. "Come, child, you may help me pack the basket."

Angela, sent upstairs to don cooler clothing for the *fête champêtre,* came down soon after looking as fine as fivepence in a new rose-sprigged muslin Maggie had made her. As she entered the kitchen, she marveled at Maggie's industry, and began to help her hostess pack up the picnic lunch. As she surveyed the lavish spread, "Are we preparing to feed an army, or to stay at the ruined monastery for several days?" she teased, her pleasure in the *al fresco* treat very obvious.

Maggie smiled. "Ye must have observed that

101

Rrrrichard has a hearty appetite," she offered, getting out a second, smaller hamper for the liquid refreshments. "He'll have the gig at the door any minute now. I must bustle up and change my gown!"

Impatient to begin the holiday, Angela carried the huge hamper to the front door. Just as she reached it, she heard a staccato knocking. Carefully setting down her burden upon the broad hall seat, Angela opened the door. Two young ladies, very formally dressed for such an early morning visit, gave back her stare of surprise.

"We have come to call upon Miss Bennet," said the younger and prettier of the two; then added, smiling roguishly, "and her brother."

The older girl, handsome rather than beautiful, was subjecting Angela to a hard, assessing scrutiny. She spoke very coldly. "Well, girl, are your wits gone begging? Tell your master he has guests!"

The younger woman frowned as she glanced from Angela's charmingly modish gown to her sister's scornful face.

"Addie," she remonstrated, "surely this is not—"

"Not a servant?" snapped Addie. "Well, why is she opening Richard's door, then?"

Angela might have appeared guileless, but she was neither meek nor stupid. "I am a guest here—" she began with some hauteur, and then interrupted the intended setdown as she remembered the circumstances in which she had been brought to Bennet Farm—more like a lost kitten rescued from drowning than an honored, invited guest.

Addie noted her hesitation. "Yes? You are a guest, you say? Of Miss Bennet's, or of Daisy Fowler's? My mother tells us that young Daisy is working here as a maid."

"Addie!" This time the younger girl was openly shocked at her sister's unpleasant manner. "We are the Dolbees, ma'am. I am Eunice and this is my sister Adella. Our father is a lawyer in London, and brings us to Crofton village when the Courts are in recess. We have a manor house near Crofton—"

But this was too much easy civility to suit Adella Dolbee. "Is this chit to keep us nattering upon the doorstep forever?" she demanded. "Take us to Richard Bennet, girl, and then you can get on with your work," and she glanced meaningfully at the hamper on the hall seat.

The situation was saved by the approach of Maggie Bennet. It cannot be said that her face lighted up with pleasure at sight of the visitors, but she greeted them with a quiet courtesy which had the effect of restraining the sneering arrogance of the elder girl.

"Do come in, Miss Dolbee and Miss Eunice! Have you met our guest Miss Swann, of Swanholme in Averly?" As she spoke, she was lead-

103

ing the visitors into the parlor and indicating seats. "And how are your parents? I trust they are well?"

"Mamma and Pappa are well, ma'am," answered Addie. "Mamma instructed me to convey her greetings to you, and to urge you to call upon us at Dolbee Manor."

"Thank Mrs. Dolbee for me," replied Maggie. Angela noticed with rather unworthy satisfaction that she made no definite commitment.

Miss Eunice was staring unashamedly at Angela. "It will be such fun having you in the neighborhood, Miss Swann!" she bubbled. "I swear it is deadly dull hereabouts—no Assemblies, no great Balls, just prosy dinner parties with the youngest guests older than my sister Addie!"

"That will be quite enough, Eunice!" snapped Miss Dolbee. "You are fortunate to be permitted to attend the dinner parties, and you not out of the schoolroom yet!"

"I am to be presented in the Fall!" boasted Eunice. "Have you made your debut yet, Miss Swann?"

From the sneer on Addie's face it was easy to deduce what she thought the answer to that question must be, but Angela did not rise to the challenge. She contented herself with a quiet, "My mother is just recently dead, and I shall be going on very quietly for some time."

Beyond conventional murmurs of condolence,

there was little which could be said in answer to this, and conversation lagged. The entrance of Richard at this moment brought a revivifying element to the stiffly social atmosphere, as well as to Miss Dolbee's fine eyes. Angela found herself experiencing a pang of jealousy so severe that it startled her.

In spite of some not-so-subtle hints from her younger sister, Addie refused to take her leave. Since she addressed her whole attention to Richard, the latter, impatient to take his Angela on the picnic, finally said, "Did my sister tell you we are showing our guest the ruined abbey today?"

Eunice spoke up before her sister had a chance to reply to the question. "Oh, a picnic! What fun you will have! We never do anything interesting like that." She pouted. "It is so dull here in the country that I swear I wish we had never left London!"

For once Addie did not seem to wish to repress her sister, or scold her for hoydenish behavior. Instead she looked at Richard with direct inquiry.

After the merest moment of hesitation, Richard responded courteously. "Would you care to join us then, Addie and Eunice? I am convinced my sister will have packed enough for a dozen. She believes I am a hearty trencherman!"

So it was with the greatest discontent upon the part of at least two of the members of the group, five persons set out for the site of the promised treat. Richard had very firmly handed up the Misses Dolbee into their own smart little gig, and saw them started down the lane, before he turned to assist Maggie and Angela to mount into his carriage.

"Ye'll note ma wily stratagem," he chuckled, but his eyes were intent upon the sober countenance of Angela. "Ah didna offer to take us all in one carriage. This way, the ladies from the Manor will no' be forced to come back to the Farm wi' us—an' maybe maneuver an invitation to dinner oot o' ma softhearted sister!"

The man's expression lightened as Angela smiled in response to his teasing, and he set the gig rolling merrily along the lane after the aforesaid ladies from the Manor.

Angela was wishing with all her heart that they had been well upon their way before the Dolbees arrived. It was obvious to her that the senior Miss Dolbee had her sights firmly fixed upon one Richard Bennet, Gentleman Farmer, and would have no scruples in fighting to achieve her objective. Could Angela make a contest of it? Did she even wish to? Rather to her own surprise, she discovered that she did very strongly desire to enter such a skirmish—and to win it! Her present emotions: anger, disappointment, jealousy, fierce possessiveness, were so foreign to her usual modes of feeling that she knew she would have to come to terms with them. She must make a fight for her own happiness.

Richard cast several questioning glances at the girl who sat so quietly beside him. He was regretting that her earlier open delight in the expedition seemed to have disappeared. He cursed himself for the slavish obedience to social custom which had forced him to issue the invitation to the Dolbees, and hoped devoutly that he could manage to get Angela to himself for even a few precious moments sometime during the day.

Maggie, too, was unhappy at the turn of events. What might have been the occasion for a decisive advance in her plans for Richard and Angela had now to be considered a wasted day. Drat the Dolbee girl! Every time she came to Crofton she found many excuses to appear at Bennet Farm, and Maggie's great dolt of a brother was too blind to see what the minx was about! Maggie fumed silently, considering methods of getting rid of the intruders.

So it was a silent trio which reached the environs of the old abbey half an hour later. The scene was attractive. The massive gray stone blocks of which the building had originally been constructed had been so long abandoned to the depredations of local barn-builders that the remnants no longer defined the shape of the great refectory and the small cells, but lay about in an interesting disarray, while green turf and small flowering bushes made a charming maze out of the old ruins.

Posing picturesquely upon the most prominent of the many blocks, the Dolbee sisters presented a pretty, if somewhat artificial tableau. Angela thought them quite too beautiful, and hated them in smiling silence. Maggie Bennet, less directly concerned, decided to become more actively involved.

"Very picturesque," she said briskly, deflating Addie's pretensions of artlessness. "Now if you will help me to set out the collation, girls, we shall allow Richard to deal with the horses."

Since it was now observed that Addie, in her haste to set the scene romantically, had neglected to make any provision for her horses' comfort or security, Richard was soon occupied in settling both teams in the shade. With a rather poor grace, the elder Miss Dolbee descended from her perch and strolled over to the spot Maggie had chosen, beneath a spreading oak tree, to set out the repast. The younger Dolbee was happy enough to assist Angela and her bright chatter kept the occasion from degenerating into gloomy silence.

After the meal, whose tempting excellence considerably lightened everyone's mood, Richard rose, stretched lazily, and grinning at Angela, said hopefully, "While the other ladies rest, perhaps Miss Swann would permit me to redeem my promise to show her around the ruins?"

He found that in Miss Addie he was dealing with a seasoned campaigner. "Oh, yes, let us permit Richard to give us the Grand Tour, Miss Swain. I can assure you he is most competent, and knows all the most delightful secret nooks!" She moved over to place her hand upon Richard's sleeve, and cast him a very languishing look.

Ignoring the insult implicit in her rival's "Miss Swain," Angela digested the implications present in "delightful secret nooks." What visions that conjured up! Torn between chagrin and jealousy, Angela was about to refuse to accompany them when a sharp jab in her back from Maggie warned her not to be missish. Gasping, she got to her feet and walked to Richard's other side, encouraged by the warmth of his welcoming smile.

Richard might have been a gentleman, but he was no slow-top. Instead of offering his arm to Angela, he took her hand firmly in his big one and then tucked her forearm against his side. Together the reluctant threesome strolled about among the stone blocks and shrubbery for quite half an hour before Addie conceded defeat and strode back to the oak tree beneath which Maggie sat, guarding the hampers and the sleeping Miss Eunice. Everyone was willing to concede that the picnic was over. Richard spent the next few minutes reharnessing both teams and handing the Dolbee ladies into their gig. With many falsely bright expressions of gratitude and pleasure, Miss Addie drove off, with Eunice perched apprehensively beside her.

"Phew!" sighed Richard, wiping his brow with elaborate care. "In future, Maggie, if you see me about to do the pretty to any of our neighbors, will ye kindly put a dishclout in ma mouth?"

Angela and Maggie had to chuckle at his lugubrious expression, and Maggie remarked that she would be more than pleased to accommodate him. So the party rode back to Bennet Farm, and although all three regretted the Dolbee invasion, Maggie was able to announce that she was much restored by her brief holiday from domesticity.

A few days later, sitting companionably beside her hostess as they mended table linen, Angela ventured upon her first personal question.

"Have you and Richard lived at Bennet Farm a long time?"

"Not as such things are reckoned here," Maggie answered, nipping off a thread with her teeth. "The place was given to my father when we came down from the Scottish estates to serve the old Lord Elsingham. I was a young girl, nurse to the Laird's little son, him that's the present Laird. My parents farmed this land, and when they died it became Richard's and mine. And a fine thing he has made of it—the best holding in the district!" she added with simple pride.

110

It had to be said. Angela asked shyly, "Does Richard have—is your brother—is he planning to be married soon?"

Maggie shot a quick glance at the girl's rosy, down-bent face and then became very busy threading a needle. "Not just at the moment, he is not, although there are signs . . . yes, I'd say definite signs." She thought of the violet-covered hat and the ghost of a smile quirked on her lips.

"What is the—the lady's name?" pursued Angela doggedly. Better far to know the worst at once, and school her foolish heart. When Maggie didn't speak, Angela asked, "Has Richard's lady come to visit while I have been here?"

There had been a few callers, but Angela did not think any of the female ones the right age or sufficiently attractive to deserve so noble, so fascinating, so loveable a man as Richard Bennet. Something of this showed in her open countenance, for Maggie took a long look at the expressive little face and nodded with satisfaction.

"I see I can confide in you," she began with an air at once friendly and furtive. "My brother, I must admit, is a very romantic man. Under that dour Scots phlegm dwells a soul of fire and derring-do, a heart—" abandoning abruptly her flight of oratory, Maggie concluded with a conspiratorial smile, "—a heart as soft as a pudding! Angela, my dear, you are a woman. You must

111

have seen through Richard's male reserve to the warmhearted boy who lives inside?"

"He has been everything that is gentle, good and kind to me," agreed Angela devoutly.

"He once loved a very beautiful woman who, though she accepted his help in a dangerous matter, and truly valued him, was already pledged to another man. Richard served this lady well, and believed himself to be totally committed to her, even though he well knew the lady loved her husband, and that he himself could neither expect nor receive anything but her gratitude."

The girl's eyes were wide with pity and wonder. That this charming, cheerful, handsome giant should be hiding a broken heart! Angela longed to be the one to bring comfort to him, to enrich his life as he had enriched hers!

"Who was this lady?" she whispered, all her feelings clearly revealed in her expression.

"It was Milady Nadine Elsingham, she who is now wishful to be called Kathryn. They are not always in residence at the Manor, but when they are, they always invite Richard and me to dine, to celebrate old loyalties."

"I should think a man as proud as Richard would rather stay away," said Angela shortly and, if truth be told, jealously. What kind of a woman was this who kept reminding a brave man of his bootless love? "Does she *know?*"

Correctly interpreting this rather obscurely

worded question, Maggie said gently, "She knows that Richard believed himself to be in love with her. She also knows that never, by word or deed, would he refer to it. He is a proud man, Angela, as well as a worthy one."

Angela was not appeased. Anyone who, having seen Richard Bennet, could settle for a lesser man, was foolish beyond permission and thus unworthy of consideration. But there was a question which still had to be asked. It was the most difficult one of all. The girl drew a deep breath. "Does he—does Richard still—" She could not say it.

Maggie Bennet took three more stitches. Her face revealed nothing of the thoughts which bubbled in her shrewd, elderly mind. Then she said quietly, "I do not think Richard is still as passionately devoted to Milady as once he was. After all, it has been five years! But if one dared to ask him about it, which I could not, I think he might say, quite honestly, that the old spell still endured. Men are creatures of habit, my dear, and once having taken an attitude, find it hard to change." She sighed. "It is more than a pity, it is a crying shame that so fine a man should not enjoy the love and comfort of a wife and family in his middle age."

Angela rose to a rebuttal as fiercely as Maggie had hoped. " 'Middle age'?" she challenged. "Richard Bennet is as young and strong and— and attractive as any man I have ever seen! He is—he is—" the girl was suddenly aware of what she was revealing, and subsided in red-cheeked embarrassment. After a long moment during which neither woman spoke, Angela said quietly, "Miss Bennet, can you forgive me for that unseemly outburst? And *please* not tell your brother what I said?"

Maggie, well content with events so far, was quite willing to give her assurances.

"Let us go into the kitchen now and bake Richard a nut-and-raisin cake with spices. It is his favorite sweet."

But Angela was still digesting the unpalatable news she had been given. "I think, perhaps, dear Miss Bennet, that I should be seeking for steady employment. It has been truly wonderful to be your guest and Richard's—" her soft voice stumbled over the name—"but you know I was running away from any security I ever had when I left Swanholme. I must have work and wages to keep my pride intact."

Maggie considered this, frowning. Had she wrought worse than she hoped in explaining Richard's lost love to this girl? Had it been a piece of pernicious meddling? Old fool that she was, she had wanted the girl to fight for her love, not run away! And now there was the business of finding employment rearing its head again. Maggie "set her mouth stubborn," as her mother had been wont to say.

"Angela, there is something which I have

114

been reluctant to tell you." She paused significantly.

The girl rose to the bait like any salmon. She clasped her slender hands, her eyes wide and fearful. "Oh, what is it, Miss Bennet?"

"I am not at all well," began Maggie mendaciously. "It has been suggested that I slacken off—" *May I be forgiven!* thought the older woman, who had never needed nor desired to slacken off in all her active, healthy life, "—but I am reluctant to leave Richard with all the trouble and drudgery of house management, for he has the farm business to superintend, and—" she paused, apparently overcome by the mere thought of Richard's inevitable problems, but actually because her imagination had failed to supply any further details of this barefaced deceit. *And I only hope the child won't run straight to Richard with offers to help, and expose the whole plot!* thought Maggie grimly.

To avoid such a disaster, the old woman went on, "Dear Angela, we must neither of us speak of *anything* which we have discussed this afternoon! Richard would at once insist that he should handle both farm and house, and would throw himself quickly into resolving all our problems—mine and yours. You see," she added truthfully, "he has been told nothing of *my* difficulties, nor do I wish him to hear what I have shared with you."

Angela quite saw that it would be impossible

to prevent Richard from taking over completely at even a hint of his beloved sister's illness. Then a truly wonderful idea came to the girl, one which accorded so completely with her own desires as to be almost magically *right*. "Dear Miss Bennet—dear Maggie—you must permit me to remain and be your housekeeper, maid-servant, cook, whatever is needed! Oh, can you not see how truly *meant* it was that I should have been brought to you just at this time? That I have had a week to watch your ways and familiarize myself with your home? Please say that I may stay here to serve you for as long as you need me!"

Maggie had a guilty feeling that she had played a trick on both the girl and Richard, but since it was in such a worthy cause, and for their own eventual happiness, she prudently resolved to feel no remorse for her manipulations. Sighing as one relieved of an intolerable burden, she gave Angela a loving smile and took her outstretched hand.

"Dear child," she said, "you can have no idea how your wonderful generosity touches my heart!" Then, before anything could happen to spoil the plan, or cause the girl to change her mind, Maggie said quickly, "Of course I accept your offer! But the circumstances must remain our secret—promise me! I shall just tell Richard I have persuaded you to stay and help me with my housekeeping. The dear man will be delighted. He likes you."

Hoping against the odds that it might be so, Angela went cheerfully out to the kitchen to steep a fresh pot of tea for her new employer. To Maggie's surprise, she did everything exactly as Miss Bennet herself was wont to do, and the excellent brew which resulted could in no way be told apart from Miss Bennet's own concoction. It seemed to the older woman that Heaven had smiled upon her benevolent deception.

Chapter 9

AT dinner that evening Richard received the news of the hiring of Angela as housekeeper a little quizzically. He kept glancing from one to the other of the ladies as though trying to understand something which should not have needed puzzling out. He did not make any comment except to express approval of the new relationship. Both ladies were pleased with their skill in deception. So pleased was Angela that she did not think to be nervous when Richard invited her to stroll around the Home Farm after dinner.

She joined him happily, appreciating the time spent in his company, and sharing his pleasure in the well-run enterprise. The man led her to a little rise beyond the main buildings, and halted with her under the shade of an ancient tree. Wordlessly he pointed to the broad, fair expanse before them, falling away in patchwork shapes of green in many different shades, each field neatly bordered by the darker green of hedges.

In the sunset, the rolling countryside took on a glow of golden peace. Angela caught a breath of delight.

"I have never seen anything more lovely!" she said softly.

The man's eyes were fixed upon her face. "Nor have I," he said, huskily.

Angela's startled gaze met his intent one.

"Why did you decide to stay?" he demanded. "Is it because of—me?" He cupped his big hands around her shoulders firmly.

"Please . . . you must not ask me," the girl faltered. They were so close that she could feel the warmth of his body.

"Why must I not?" Richard demanded. "Is it too soon?"

"Oh, yes! Too soon!" echoed Angela, her wits gone begging.

Richard scanned her rosy face and trembling body with considerable discontent. He tightened his grip on her shoulders. "I have never felt the need to learn the rules of dalliance, and you obviously are too young and innocent to know the proper procedures," he said in a voice of dissatisfaction. "It is clearly a case of the blind leading the blind."

Angela, prey at once to rapture and alarm, could only nod wordlessly, her great eyes fixed with painful intensity upon the beloved face.

"I believe I had better kiss you," decided Richard. "I am very sure such a gesture would be perfectly *comme il faut*—given our situation and the natural beauty which surrounds us."

"Quite *comme il faut*," agreed Angela in a strangled voice.

Suddenly Richard favored her with his devastating smile. "I am a great fool—and you, my dear, are a small one," he chuckled. "Come here! I wish to kiss you—and be damned to propriety, etiquette, and Mrs. Grundy!" At which point Richard bent his head and kissed Angela.

It was a long, hard, hot kiss. Perhaps it lacked subtlety and skill; certainly it lacked elegance, but to Angela it was the most thrilling experience of her whole eighteen years. It was a completely satisfying method of communication between two persons, she decided—if they were the right two persons. The girl could not understand why Richard had not so communicated with her before. Time spent in other, lesser, activities seemed to her to constitute a singular waste of opportunity. She gave herself up to communicating with all the enthusiasm of her heart. Since she forgot, in the exigency of the moment, to take a breath, she was gasping and dizzy when Richard finally released her mouth. She staggered a little within his loosened grasp.

Richard was also experiencing an unaccustomed vertigo. He felt the ground move a little beneath his well-shod feet, and even reeled before he got his balance. He drew a wondering breath. "I had not understood that kissing had that effect," he murmured. "I seem to be intoxicated!" He stared down into the flowerlike, dazed countenance of his companion. "I had better get us both home while we can still navigate."

"That would be *comme il faut*," agreed the girl in a voice of wonder.

The trip back to the Farm was accomplished in silence.

Disaster struck the following day.

Early in the morning, before either Maggie or Angela had come down to the kitchen, Richard was up and away to the nearest small market town to arrange for shipments of his special crop of berries, just coming into maturity. The ladies partook of a leisurely breakfast prepared by young Daisy Fowler, a bright and capable farmgirl Maggie was training as a cook. Immediately after the meal, Maggie announced that she would instruct Daisy, and Angela too, if she wished, in the arcane Scottish art of making haggis.

Daisy was highly amused at this bit of national self-deception. When challenged as to the reason for her mirth, the girl giggled, "It's true ye're known throughout the district as a prime cook, Mistress Bennet, for all ye're a foreigner, but 'aggis is an English dish! My granny taught me that dish years ago, and said she had it from *her* gran!"

"Then you'd better demonstrate your skill—or your grandmother's—immediately," snapped Maggie, but there was a twinkle in her eye. "Here's the lungs, heart and liver of a calf; there's fine oatmeal and spices and suet; and a stout board to chop 'em all on. Make us your English 'aggis!"

Daisy got smartly to work, deputing minor tasks to the other two women with fine authority. The three were soon happily absorbed in their work, and quite unaware of the heavy traveling coach which came along the lane and drew up in front of the farmhouse door. A heavyset man alighted and, marching up to the front door, began to beat a thunderous fusillade upon the knocker.

Frowning, Maggie started for the front hall.

"Let me go," Angela offered. She had been sifting spices, and her hands were dry and clean. "If it's nothing important, I can save you a trip."

As Maggie looked at her suety hands, there was a renewed battering. "Nothing important?" she quoted the girl. "That racket sounds like the crack of doom!"

Prophetic words.

Angela opened the door crossly, prepared to repel some bumptious traveler. Gilles Loring grinned down at her in triumph. Before she could recover from the shock of seeing him, he

123

had stepped inside the door and seized her wrist in his heavy hand.

"You've led me quite a chase, my dear," he said, twisting her wrist just enough to remind her of earlier pain. "If you come with me now, very quietly, and cause me the minimum of trouble, I may not beat you very hard."

Angela stared at him, frightened out of speech or coherent thought.

Into the ensuing silence Maggie's voice came clearly. "What is it, Angela? Do you need me?"

"Do you, my dear?" asked Gilles, twisting a little harder.

"It is—it is my stepfather," Angela's voice came out of her mouth in a kind of croak. Her anguished gaze slid up to Gilles's face, and caught an expression of satisfaction upon it. Evidently it did not occur to him that his victim might have confided in the woman to whom she was now speaking. Angela had never discussed with any of the servants or her mother's friends the punishments she had had to endure at Gilles's hands; it would have been an agonizing embarrassment for the girl to confess her terror and revulsion, and he knew it. He smiled down at her.

Then Maggie Bennet was in the hallway with them, her small elderly body as stiff and poised for aggressive action as a mother cat's. Angela was afraid lest her new employer, openly defying Loring, might bring upon herself the kind of reprisal he was only too eager to make to women defenseless and alone in the house. But Maggie surprised both Angela and Gilles Loring.

"Oh, is this your stepfather, then? Welcome, Squire Loring! Angela has told us of your wonderful care of her father's estate! Come in and let us offer you a drink. It must be dusty work on the roads!" Her manner displayed a fawning servility which had Angela's eyes wide with shock. Gilles, having never met his hostess, could not be aware of the falsity of her manner, but there was no doubt he was reassured by it.

"And you," he said with his pompously jovial address, "must be the good woman who has sheltered my poor disturbed daughter."

"I am sure it was grief for her dear mamma which caused her to run away from her childhood home, sir," said Maggie, very mealy-mouthed. "It is often thus with young girls at a time of stress."

"Whatever her reasons, she has put me to a great deal of trouble," answered Gilles, turning upon Angela a look which promised that he would even the score. "I have come to take her back to her home. I hope she will not seek to cause any more difficulties for me, or for *you,* ma'am, who has been—*kind* enough to shelter the runaway!"

There was open threat in that remark, and Angela lost color. Gilles knew her well enough

125

to be sure she would not wish to cause trouble for any woman who had been good to her.

Maggie smoothed over the threatening moment. "Well, sir, it is just on dinnertime, for we keep country hours at Bennet Farm. You must stay and break your fast with us, for I'll be bound it is long enough since you ate, and that, most like, a rough tavern meal, quite unfit for the Squire of Swanholme!"

Torn between annoyance at the thought of delay and complacence at the flattering welcome of the plump little woman, Gilles Loring allowed himself to be persuaded to play off his dust with a glass of Richard Bennet's finest brandy while he awaited the promised meal.

"It will give Angela time to pack her belongings, and you an opportunity to refresh yourself. Angela, take your stepfather up to the guest room and be sure it is well provided with fresh water and towels."

She soon had all of them moving to her directions, even the formidable Mr. Loring. Although he was by nature a suspicious man, Gilles could see no way in which one old woman, a kitchen-maid, and his stepdaughter could harm him or prevent him and the two stout fellows he had on the box of his carriage from doing or taking whatever they wished. He had learned from the ostler at the George and Horse Inn at Crofton that Mr. Richard Bennet was away to Pilbury to hawk his fine berries at that small market town. It was unlikely he would return before dusk, for there was a fair there, and the liquor would be flowing. So the coast was clear. He'd eat the old woman's food and watch Angela and let her worry about what he had in store for her.

His suspicions were further lulled by the fact that the old biddy had made no effort to keep the girl away from him; had, in fact, sent her to show him to the guest room. He followed her slender form as she silently led the way up a wide, well-polished staircase to a roomy and surprisingly elegant second story. Gilles noted the well-kept floors, the neat carpets, the painted walls and doors, and then the nicely furnished room to which he was led.

"Your room, my dear?" he smiled insinuatingly.

Angela's expression was blank. "I am the housekeeper," she avoided his question.

He closed the door, caught her wrist, and drew her to him. "You had a good run, little vixen, but I've got you safe now."

"The wash basin, ewer and soap are there on the commode," Angela pointed to a neat walnut stand. "Towels on the rack."

Gilles was angry at her cool composure. He twisted her arm until she whimpered deep in her throat.

"I warn you I shall put up with no more of your whims and defiant starts. It was bad enough coping with your mother's megrims. You, my girl, will henceforth do exactly as I bid you, or, by God, you will rue it!"

Angela nodded, white-faced. He held her with his glare for several moments, testing her subservience. Then he strode over to the commode.

"You may wait here while I wash," he jibed, and laughed as Angela scuttled out the door and closed it softly after her.

The girl was thinking in a kind of frenzy of fear and hatred. She knew she should be logical, calm, sensible, or she would never be able to escape the fate which seemed at this minute to be inevitable. She thought wildly of casting herself down the stairwell, but could not overcome the fear that she would only receive major injuries rather than the escape of death. To be crippled and at Gilles's mercy was too hideous an image to be endured! It seemed to Angela that if she wished to run away, now was the best time. Yet could she accomplish an escape? Gilles had most likely stationed his men in sight of both front and back entrances to the farmhouse, and she would be caught before she could leave the farm.

Why had Maggie Bennet acted as she did? Maggie was firmly loyal to those she counted friends. She knew Angela's story, and had been quick in offering sympathy and help to the girl. Then it must be a ploy of some nature, a plan for outwitting Loring, this effusive hospitality!

What could the plan be? The insistence upon the meal suggested that Maggie might have some idea of serving the unwelcome visitor with a sleeping potion, to enable Angela to slip away. But Gilles's menservants? Well, they could be given a glass of ale as easily as their master!

Her musings were interrupted by the appearance of Gilles Loring in the hallway. "You may escort me downstairs now," he smiled. With a sinking of heart, Angela did so.

They were just finishing a leisurely nuncheon, enlivened by a bottle of Richard Bennet's best brandy, when there was the sound of a scuffle in the kitchen, the door of the dining room opened, and Richard Bennet himself strolled in, breathing a little heavily but very serene of manner. His first glance was toward Angela. The joyful shock on her face assured him that everything Daisy had gasped out when she found him at Pilbury market was true.

Sent off by Maggie to fetch her master home, the maid had ridden hell-for-leather, and found Mr. Bennet exactly where Maggie had said he would be. Richard had set out at once for the farm, breaking all local records for the distance. On arrival, he had encountered Gilles's servants, one at the barn, easily overcome by a single blow. The other, gorging himself in the kitchen, had put up a slightly better show, but the final result was never in question.

And now Richard, who had prepared his strategy on the road, strode forward and offered his hand to the gaping Loring. The latter, in the act of rising to confront the newcomer, was put off balance by Richard's gesture of welcome, and found himself eased back into his seat by a grip which startled and dismayed him.

Next Richard kissed his sister's cheek and announced in a cheerful voice, "I made such an excellent compact with the stall-keepers at Pilbury that I hurried back to start the men picking and crating the baskets of berries. But enough of business. I doubt that Squire Loring will find it of interest. How did you find us, by the way?"

Gilles, anticipating no opposition from this simple farmer, explained that his nephew, heartbroken at the sudden defection of his bride-to-be, had taken stage for London. When his coach stopped for a change of horses at the Pride of Exeter, he had been shocked to behold his erstwhile fiancée the center of a common brawl in the courtyard, with accusations of theft being freely bandied about, and the Law invoked.

"So of course," said Richard smoothly, "he at once leaped down to the defense of his bride-to-be?"

Gilles was as disconcerted as though a playful puppy had sprung at his throat. He took another, more carefully assessing, look at the bucolic simpleton before he said, angrily, "The coach was drawing out of the yard as he recognized his intended in the disgraceful apparel of the accused female. He had to wait until the next coach stop before he could get out and board another which returned him to me at Swanholme."

Richard interrupted the tirade, but with so mild a tone and visage that Gilles was momentarily disarmed. "Swanholme? That's Angela's family estate, is it not? Shall you wish to be married from there, my love?"

This question served to silence every person in the room. Gilles's mouth fell open, and for a frozen moment he was not able to think beyond the devastating implications of the question which had been tossed so lightly into the conversation. Maggie's eyes opened wide, and her eyebrows rose to the neat white fringe of hair on her forehead. The girl stared at Richard, and up from her slender throat swept a tide of clear color which gave her delicate features a rare beauty. Then an irresistible smile parted the soft lips, and her gray eyes sparkled like jewels. From somewhere—her love of the speaker, her fear of Gilles—she was able to draw the courage and quickness of wit needed to back Richard's play.

"But of course, dear Richard," she said demurely, tempering her delighted smile to a maidenly simper, "it is my own father's beloved home. And I know Mr. Loring would wish it so, as well, for he is widely respected in the county, and is known as a thoughtful and generous stepfather. He has guarded and enriched my estate by his careful husbandry. It will be his triumph to demonstrate to your noble sponsor what wonders he has wrought with my father's diminished holding."

As she completed this fulsome speech, made to give Richard some ideas, and time to plot his next step, Angela wondered if in fact she might have been a little too fulsome to a man who knew the dread and horror with which she regarded him. Still, Gilles Loring was guided, in public at least, by what his neighbors expected of him, and would surely put on a show if forced into it.

She sadly underrated her stepfather. His face red with anger, he turned upon the girl. "What bloody nonsense is this? You are engaged to Vivian Nellis, girl—and lucky that he finds himself willing to keep the contract after your infamous behavior!" He glared at Maggie and Richard. "Do you know that this—this hoyden flaunted herself at a public inn wearing a garment which outraged common decency? That she was accused of stealing some nobleman's jewels? She is fortunate indeed that I do not commit her to a nunnery!"

"But how sad to lose her estate to the church," suggested Richard calmly. "I feel sure wiser counsel will prevail."

"So you know about that, do you?" snarled Gilles. "Why, you cheap fortune hunter, I'll—"

Richard again interrupted his guest. "Hardly a fortune hunter, Mr. Loring. You may ask our local magistrate, Lord Elsingham, as to my position in the county, and my credit. I own this farm, which has a considerable value, several other pieces of property, and a small house in Edinburgh. Lord Elsingham will be pleased to vouch for me, if it comes to a question of my net worth."

Angela dared to offer another comment. "But that is much more than Vivian has, is it not, Mr. Loring?"

"I'll permit no damned Scots rebel to marry into my family," blustered Gilles.

"Rebels is exactly what we were not," Richard advised him. ' 'My father was a friend of the old Lord Elsingham, and came out for the English in the late disturbance. For which reason my family emigrated to England."

"She's promised to my nephew—" shouted Gilles.

Angela interrupted. "Did you not tell us that Vivian was so unhappy with my behavior that he returned to Swanholme to tattle rather than setting out at once to rescue me from the persecutions I was forced to undergo? It is no thanks to him that I am not dead or—or ravished! Had it not been for Mr. Bennet's chivalry and good-

133

will, I might have been forever lost!" Overcome by her emotions, Angela burst into tears.

While this public display of female instability disconcerted Loring, Richard, that pawky Scot, took it in stride. Rising at once, he went to his supposed fiancée and put a supportive arm around her. Under the guise of murmuring soothing words, he whispered, "Doing it a bit too brown, dear!" and hugged her gently. Then aloud he said, "Maggie, will you take dear Angela to her room and sit with her until the tone of her mind had been restored? I believe that only a woman can offer the proper consolation and attentions at such a time. You will know what soothing potions are needed to calm her very natural perturbation of spirit."

His hearers gazed at the huge Scot as he wove his careful wall of protection between the girl and her stepfather. Maggie was struck with awe and wonder at this masterful performance. She hastened to do his bidding, carefully ushering a still-weeping Angela out of the dining room and up the stairs.

Richard, who had stood while the ladies left the room, walked over to the sideboard and poured two large glasses full of Scotch whiskey for his guest and himself.

Loring accepted the liquor and drained the glass. His narrowed gaze attested to the fact that he understood that a man like Richard Bennet, with his wide, fertile acres, his houses, his hard blue eyes, and above all with his claim of close friendship with a well-known peer, was a tougher customer than Gilles had been used to dealing with this last five years. No bucolic gape-seed, he; nor impecunious parson nor fat country squire fuddled with drink, who could be choused or flattered into doing whatever Loring wanted. This Bennet was an awkward customer indeed, and to fend him off from seizing the whole estate would require some pretty fancy footwork. In short, this was disaster for Gilles Loring, unless he could figure a way to come about quickly. In an open duel, with its attendant publicity, certain facts about Loring's past might be revealed which could ruin him completely.

So Gilles put on his bluff, hearty mask and said, with the false bonhomie which had fooled so many of his Averly neighbors, "Well, Mr. Bennet, I can see you are a serious suitor for my stepdaughter, not some lecherous nobleman or encroaching country bumpkin. We shall have to consider you seriously. Why do you not return with us to Swanholme, and let us get closer acquainted with you? Then, when we are sure Angela knows her own mind, and I am satisfied with the settlements, we can announce the banns . . ." and he gave his imitation of a smile. *Once I get her home, I'll fix it.*

Richard's more than matched it in width and falsity.

135

"That's unco' gude an' generous o' ye, Mr. Loring," Richard said, of a sudden very Scottish, "but Ah'm afeared there'll no be time for you an' me to get better acquainted. You see Angela and I are gettin' married in three days' time. By special license." (And the Lord forgive me for the lies I've told this day, but all in good cause, he thought.)

"Three days!" Loring, put off balance by his host's sudden lapse into the vernacular, was quite astounded at the news. Rage began to build in him—at Angela, at his stupid, undependable nephew, at Fate, but most of all at this frustrating, round-eyed Scot with his unbelievable presumption and his massive, powerful body. Not one to be lightly intimidated, this Richard Bennet.

Perhaps Gilles Loring had lorded it too long over frail, cowed females, servants well paid to do his bidding, and beef-witted country squires who admired his hard laughter and drive. He could not accept that he had been outfaced by a slip of a girl whom he had expected to torment and enjoy at his leisure, and by her canny schemer of a Scottish farmer. He sprang to his feet and advanced upon the interloper.

Angela had been confident of Richard's ability to deal with even so formidable an antagonist as her wicked stepfather. Her faith was justified during the next few minutes, when her champion provided a classic example of cross and jostle which would have brought cheers at Cribb's or Gentleman Jackson's. In fact, Gilles, a pretty good rough-and-tumble man in his youth, was himself taken completely by surprise. Before he could get in a single effective blow he found himself supine, his dazed vision helplessly fixed upon the stout black beams of the dining room ceiling. Hauled none too gently to his feet by an iron grip upon the nape of his neck, he was obliged to accept this rude persuasion to move out of the dining room and into the hall. There, still dazed, he felt his hat placed firmly upon his head and his person propelled ruthlessly through the front door and out to his own carriage, which by some miracle appeared before the doorway. Upon the box sat his coachman and groom, both looking the worse for wear. With a single mighty heave, which impressed Gilles even in his dreamily detached state, Richard Bennet thrust him into the coach and closed the door firmly after him.

"You may drive your master back to Swanholme," Richard said quietly. "When he is ready to listen, inform him that my wife and I shall call upon him there after our honeymoon."

"I wager neither of us'll be around, come that day," muttered the groom to his fellow as the coach lurched down the lane. "He'll want to get rid of any who saw him lookin' like that," and he cocked his thumb back toward the body of the coach.

"Sick as a horse, 'e was," agreed his mate, gloomily.

"Did ye twig that farmer?" asked the groom. "Not a hair out o' place, not even breathin' heavy, an' his nibs knocked into the middle o' next week!"

"I ain't seen nothin' an' I ain't sayin' nothin'," announced the coachman glumly. He had learned in a hard school how to survive in Gilles Loring's household.

Chapter 10

RICHARD Bennet came back into the kitchen to find three women waiting for him with varying degrees of anxiety. He was looking very well pleased with himself, and Maggie grinned in sympathy.

"I wish I had been here to see it!" she said wistfully.

Richard rubbed his knuckles with a deprecatory smile. "I am at heart a man of peace," he began piously, and then broke into a chuckle. "The puir auld limmer didn't know what hit him! Ah *did* enjoy mahsel'!"

"Richard Bennet, if you don't stop being *Scottish* this instant and explain what is happening, I'll—I'll . . ." gasped Angela.

Richard was riding high. "What will ye do, ma bonnie wee love?" he teased her, his eyes bright with laughter.

"Oh, Richard!" the girl said, smiling up at him against her will. "You know we aren't going to be married, and he's sure to come back and take me away, as soon as he can gather reinforcements."

"It'll have to be an army of lawyers, then, for I've quite decided I shall marry you as soon as I can get that special license," promised the big man, his eyes twinkling.

Angela could not believe her ears. Not only had he announced their approaching nuptials to her stepfather, but now he was going on as though they were real—and no Gilles Loring present to be impressed! A strong wave of hope and happiness surged up in her breast, and she looked to see what Maggie Bennet's response would be to this outrageous proposal.

No help there. Maggie seemed as foolish as her brother, beaming fondly on the two of them as though they were beloved children rather than a strange girl she'd scarcely had time to know, and a brother old enough to know better.

Angela felt compelled to voice a protest. "Richard, you *can't!* Your future happiness . . . your freedom . . ." babbled the girl.

Richard surveyed her with amused blue eyes. "Ye can see the puir girl's quite carried away with wonder and delight," he told his sister. He straightened his broad shoulders. "Now I must take reluctant leave of you, ladies. I have to talk to the Reverend Percy about that special license. I've no doubt the good man will have useful advice for me—if I can get his nose out of whatever book he is currently reading!"

"He'll advise you against mocking the sacrament of marriage," said Angela, in a temper, "if indeed you actually do mean to speak to him." It hurt her to hear the big Scotsman making light of so serious a matter. *For he surely did not actually intend going through with this marriage?* He hadn't ever asked her! It was all a put-on to discourage Gilles, and she thanked him for it—but, oh! if it had only been true!

Richard was smiling into her perturbed countenance with heart-catching charm. He was so much the enigmatic, pawky Scot that the girl clenched her fists.

"Compleenin' already, ma bonnie dear?" he teased. "Och, 'tis plain to see I'll be sadly henpecked, Heaven help me, what wi' a managin' sister an' a domineerin' wife in the hoose!" Mimicking great fear, Richard closed the door softly behind his broad back.

"Richard!" wailed Angela. She turned to Maggie. "Miss Bennet, this is madness! Your brother hardly knows me. We met for the first time less than a week ago, under questionable circumstances." Tears formed and spilled from her eyelids. "I know what he is trying to do. He is a kind man. But marriage! How can he make a jest of that?"

"Who says Richard is jesting?" asked Maggie.

141

Angela stared at the plump little woman through her tears. "But of course it is a jest," she began, uncertainly. "You yourself said—you told me about Lady Elsingham—his ill-fated love for that lady . . ."

"Ill-fated fiddlesticks!" snapped the older woman. "It's past time my brother put aside childish things. He's thirty-one and getting no younger. Too old, for sure, to be nursing romantic notions about blighted affections! What Richard needs is a warm, loving woman to bring him joy of heart and peace of mind—and what the Reverend Percy calls a quiver-full of children!" She nodded fiercely, her bright blue eyes so like her brother's that Angela felt a thrill of recognition and love.

The girl could hardly accept that her hostess was actually endorsing Richard's fantastical behavior. Objections to the madcap scheme thronged to her mind, to her lips, but there, strangely, they seemed to dissipate. All that came out was a shamefully weak, whispered, "Do you think he—minds very much? I know he is a great-hearted gentleman, but this involves his whole *life!* Marriage to a comparative stranger, and one he cannot—cannot—"

"Cannot love?" Maggie expressed the inexpressible. "Why not?"

Angela gabbled incoherencies.

"Hush, child," soothed the older woman, patting her shoulder gently. "I've no doubt it's all been too much for you to grasp, so bedeviled by that wicked stepfather as you have been! Come away now and we'll have a nice cup of tea and talk about the wedding."

The rest of the day went by, for Angela at least, in a blur of planning, making lists, finding simple answers for preposterous questions. After Richard returned from the vicarage, however, things seemed to settle themselves with remarkable ease, and the girl's sense of unreality was gradually replaced with incredulous hope. As she prepared for bed that night in her pretty little room, Angela drew a shuddering breath of excitement. It wasn't a dream! Nothing in her short, unhappy life had prepared her for the incredible events of this day. The sinister Gilles Loring routed! A special license to be applied for! A new, happy home with Richard and the motherly Maggie. . . .

The benison of Richard's announcement of their marriage had her so flustered that she was in bed trying to get to sleep before it struck her that he had never actually proposed, but had seemed to take it for granted that what he decided upon was the only possible course of action. In such case, unasked, could she have been said to have agreed to the marriage? Did it not require the free consent of both parties? Then with a shiver she recalled Gilles's cold determination to wed her to Vivian, willy-nilly. There had scarcely been the consent of one

143

party, freely given, in that arrangement. Vivian had needed to be coerced, even bought; Angela had not been offered a choice.

In which case, she concluded happily, Richard's one-sided decision was quite suitable, and in three days might be legal. Reassured, the girl cuddled down into the goose-feather mattress and drifted off into dreamless sleep.

Chapter 11

THE following morning, before Angela had
awakened, a message was sent to Elsingham
Manor requesting permission for Mr. Richard
Bennet to wait upon its master. Instead of the
expected assent, Milord and his Lady themselves arrived at Bennet Farm about eleven.
They came in an elegant curricle, with Lord
Elsingham handling the reins and a small tiger
perched behind. When Angela was told by Daisy
of this stirring arrival, she made haste to slip
up to her bedroom and don her only presentable
dress, the becoming redingote which Richard
had purchased for her in Exeter. Regretfully
she denied herself the support of the small
violet-covered hat—very much the thing for a
morning call in London, but quite ineligible to
receive guests at a country farm. Fortified by the
redingote and Richard's kindness in buying it,
the girl descended into Maggie Bennet's parlor to
meet the only woman Richard had ever loved.

After a single glance, she understood his enthrallment. Kathryn Elsingham was the most beautiful woman Angela had ever set eyes upon. First to catch one's attention was the glorious mane of auburn hair, which, dressed simply, was an irresistible invitation to the touch. Then lovely green eyes, by turns as brightly flashing as emeralds and as seductive as a tropic sea. A man could drown in them, Angela thought despairingly. How can he think of any other woman, groaned Angela, receiving the warmth of Kathryn's genuine interest in her fellowmen. The girl gave up the battle she had never really hoped to win. Milady was a nonpareil, as kind as she was beautiful. It did not need the adoring looks Lord Elsingham cast upon his lovely Lady, and the steady devotion in Richard Bennet's expression, to convince Angela that no other woman could take the place Kathryn Elsingham held in everyone's heart. So she smiled as bravely as she was able, and behaved just as she ought in the matter of greeting and polite conversation, while something died in her breast and left a hollow place.

Lord Elsingham was telling Richard of reports he had received from some of his tenants in Elsinghurst, that a harsh-voiced man had been making very close inquiries about Richard and the newcomer at Bennet Farm. Jonas Tilley, the innkeeper, had related to his liegelord that the stranger, sporting a bruised face, had stopped

146

in for several restorative whiskeys, and made some scurrilous remarks about Bennet's guest. This, coupled with Richard's request for an interview, had caused Milord and his Lady to call upon Lord Elsingham's old nurse and her brother—a pair they obviously held in deepest affection and esteem.

"I believe the fellow means to do you harm," advised Lord Elsingham. "He made threats to go before a magistrate to lay an information against you, and was throwing about accusations of kidnapping and duress of a minor. I was able to discount his threats when I talked to Tilley, and hope to have scotched his venom, but Kathryn and I agreed that we must confer with you at once, and put a stop to such malicious gossip."

"We have found the perfect solution to the problem," announced Richard with his charming grin. The Scottish accent was quite absent from his speech when he talked with these people. Angela drew a kind of bitter comfort from the thought that he saved his endearing burr for his intimates.

"I have requested a special license from the Bishop of the Diocese," he explained, "Angela and I will be married as soon as I receive it."

Lord Elsingham was startled into a laugh. He stared from Richard's smiling face to Angela's adorably confused one. "That is cutting the Gordian knot indeed! My congratulations!"

Lady Elsingham looked from Richard to Angela with interest and concern.

"Is this what you wish, my dear?" she asked the girl. "If it is not, we can find other ways to protect you."

Angela's heart sank. How could she tell this gracious beauty that the whole desire of her foolish heart was to become Richard Bennet's wife? That life could hold for her no greater joy than to live with him, serve and love him, as long as they both should live?

Perhaps Lady Elsingham was unusually perceptive; perhaps something in the girl's steady gaze and furiously blushing features betrayed the truth to her, for after a moment Kathryn smiled wryly.

"That was a stupid suggestion to make to a newly engaged girl," she apologized. "John, you should tell me to mind my own business!"

There was exchanged between the married lovers a glance of such deep commitment that Angela was forced to look away. She found herself staring directly into Richard Bennet's intent blue eyes, and saw on his face an expression she had not observed before. Wearily she told herself that this interview with the object of his hopeless love must be painful to him, and his gallant commitment to a runaway girl could only emphasize what he had lost.

Maggie, ever tactful, was pouring tea into the delicate porcelain cups, a gift from her nursling

Lord Elsingham, which were her pride. Daisy brought in a dish of hot scones heaped with homemade strawberry jam and clotted cream.

"You always did make the best scones in England," said Lord Elsingham greedily.

"In Scotland, too," added Richard, helping himself as generously.

Kathryn Elsingham smiled at Angela. "Do they ever think of anything but their stomachs? It is a wonder they both aren't as fat as—as—"

"Porkers?" suggested Angela, greatly daring.

"I resent that," said Richard, eyes bright and amused on Angela's face. "I see I am getting myself leg-shackled to a very sharp-tongued female!"

When Richard looked at her with that laughing countenance, Angela's heart beat faster. If she could not have his love, given long since to Lady Elsingham, then at least she could have his friendship. . . .

Then Richard did something which jolted her heart into her throat. He had seated himself by her side when he had completed his self-imposed task of passing the cups of tea. Now he turned his big body toward her, bent down, and kissed her on the lips. His mouth tasted of strawberries.

There was a startled silence which Maggie broke by asking if anyone would care for another cup of tea.

Angela wondered desperately why Richard was continuing this ruse of a happy engagement. Surely it must embarrass him in front of his guests? Of course Maggie knew it for the wily gambit it had been, to checkmate Gilles Loring, but the Elsinghams were taking it seriously. Angela realized that she would have to put things straight.

"Mr. Bennet—" she began.

Richard raised one of those handsome sandy eyebrows. "So formal, my love?" he teased.

"Richard," the girl amended, blushing ridiculously. "You should perhaps explain to—to your friends that we are not—I mean, you are just—" she subsided in confusion under the combined stares of the company.

Richard smote his forehead. "What! Already regretting our engagement, and we hardly twenty-four hours plighted?" He sighed histrionically. "I'm scarcely plighted before I'm blighted!"

Delighted laughter from everyone but the girl.

That devil! thought Angela. That tricksy, teasing, maddening Scottish devil! What mischief was he up to now? Deeply she distrusted the wicked sparkle in those wide, innocent-seeming blue eyes.

Richard addressed her in a wheedling voice. "Save my blushes by agreeing that you're going to marry me as soon as the special license can be granted. Darling Angela?"

Angela did not know where to look. Eyelids

lowered, face rosy, she said softly, "If you wish it, Richard."

It was beyond her to deny this man anything; she knew it. And so, apparently, did he.

Shortly after the toast to the happy pair, drunk in Richard's finest wine, the Elsinghams departed to set matters in train for a royal reception. "We'll invite everyone you know in the district," promised Kathryn. "And Angela, you must of course inform your friends from home. I love wedding receptions—never having had one," she added, *sotto voce*. Lord Elsingham gave her such an adoring look that Angela was forced to glance away, unable to endure that obvious sign of marital bliss.

When they had departed, the girl, avoiding Richard's eyes, turned to Maggie. "I—I seem to have a headache," she apologized. "Perhaps I had better lie down for a little while."

Clucking like a mother hen, Maggie went up with her to the pretty bedroom, helped to remove shoes and the redingote, and brought a cloth wrung out of cold water for Angela's forehead. Then, drawing the curtains against the bright sunlight, she said softly, "Richard wishes us to set out for Exeter early in the morning, so you may provide any facts the Bishop may need, and sign the papers."

"I shall not be going. I cannot!" murmured Angela.

Maggie came back to the bedside and looked down at the girl. "You don't love him?"

"He doesn't love me!" wailed the girl softly.

After a moment's silence, during which Angela removed the cool cloth from her eyes, the better to observe Miss Bennet's expression, Maggie said slowly, "I might have agreed with you until this morning. But you must see how happy he was! He hasn't smiled and joked like that in Lady Elsingham's presence ever before. It is as though he were set free of a spell . . . his own man again!"

But Angela refused to listen to that which she so much longed to hear. "How could such a green girl as I am take the place of that beautiful woman? It was plain to me that you all adore her—and naturally so, for she is the kindest, most beautiful—" the girl's voice dissolved in tears. "I must leave at once!"

"You would run away?" challenged the Scotswoman.

"What else is there for me to do?"

"It will wound his pride most deeply," answered Maggie. "When first he realized that he loved Kathryn it was not so terrible, since no one but they two had knowledge of it. But this time he has told the Elsinghams, and authorized the spreading abroad of the information throughout the district. The reception at Elsingham Manor will—"

"We must stop it!" cried Angela, pulling herself upright on the bed.

"We cannot," objected Maggie. "What excuse could we give? How would Richard feel if you told everyone you were refusing his suit at this point?"

"But I never accepted it!" protested Angela. "He never asked me!" This was the sore point. "It is he who is telling everyone!"

"And you would brand him a liar?" asked Maggie sternly.

Angela sank back upon her pillow. "I shall go to Exeter," she said. "I could not bear to hurt Richard."

Maggie left with a final comforting pat on the girl's shoulder.

"But I know I am second best with him," she thought sadly when she was alone. "I always will be."

Perhaps he feels he needs a wife, and children to inherit his acres. It was the custom, she knew, to arrange marriages for such reasons. *It is only,* she told her lonely heart, *a sensible, businesslike arrangement, which Richard, being Richard, sweetens with his courtesy and humor. Well, it will rescue me from my wretched situation. I must accept his help with what grace I can muster.*

But she wept a few tears into the cold cloth.

* * *

Striding across his pleasant fields at this moment, Richard was frowning heavily. He had a strong feeling that he had mishandled the affair this morning, but what else could he have done with all those people present? Maggie, *bless* her, whisking the girl away as soon as the Elsinghams had left, giving him no chance at all to settle the matter in private! And Lady Elsingham, asking her wretched questions just as he thought he had the business neatly in hand. "Find other ways to protect you"—indeed! Devoutly the man wished Lady Elsingham had kept her lovely mouth shut, for anyone could see the girl had withdrawn at that moment. It did not occur to Richard that the woman who had so annoyed him this morning had been the object of his sternly repressed, romantic dreams for the last five years. At this stage, he wished her in Jericho, or London, or anyplace where she could not meddle with a man's affairs. There had been the moment when he kissed Angela before them all—had that not convinced the foolish girl? Thoughts of the kiss considerably lightened his mood, and he began to picture the time when he would have her to himself, in a delightful privacy guaranteed by the special license and his ring upon her slender finger— *the ring!* He must manage to slip away for a moment during the visit to Exeter tomorrow and purchase one. Now what should it be? Lost in such fascinating considerations as this question raised, Richard strode on through his fields in a state of bliss as close as a man can get to perfect joy.

Chapter 12

THE next morning Richard drove them out in his phaeton, with the folding top down and a handsome pair of matched bays between the shafts. Maggie, attired in her best bonnet and a neat black woolen dress with a wide white muslin fichu like a ruffled shawl about her shoulders, was comfortably ensconsed on the rear seat, while Angela sat beside Richard in front. As a source of courage for this incredible mission, the girl had chosen to wear the violet-covered hat. She felt it gave her the needed touch of sophistication with the gray redingote, and had firmly rejected Daisy's offer of a broad straw bonnet to protect her delicate complexion from the strong sunlight. Go to Exeter with Richard in a straw bonnet? Her heart failed at the thought. She only hoped she did him justice, this splendid creature seated next to her!

They were very early abroad, for the road to Exeter was a long one. It was a lovely English morning. Mist was rising from the fields and meadows and curling upward among the trees. The air was dew-washed; flower scents wafted on the breeze. Angela, who had come to terms with her emotions during the night, turned a shining face up to Richard.

"I do not know why you are doing this for me, Richard, but I thank you," she said softly. "I have never been so happy in all my life!" Her beautiful gray eyes were full of light, and the man beside her held the reins more tightly, lest he take her into his arms and kiss her for all the world to see.

In truth, Angela would not have refused such a loverly gesture. She had resolved that, since Richard Bennet had been kind enough to offer to marry her to save her from her wicked stepfather, she would repay him in whatever coin he might seem to wish. After the marriage there would be her fortune, and Swanholme of course, but she was well aware that he did not need or even covet them. At the moment, her gratitude and the admission of her pleasure in his company was the least she could offer him. She peeped shyly up at him, her heart in her eyes.

The big Scotsman was dressed in an unexpectedly smart outfit of dark blue superfine coat and breeches, white stockings, a cravat of starched linen, and black, silver-buckled shoes. He had not powdered his sandy hair, but had brushed it until it shone like dull gold. On it, rather rakishly, he had set the soft dark hat which Angela knew was all the kick for country wear, because Vivian, wearing one such, had told her it had replaced the tricorne. By this time completely besotted by the big fellow, Angela decided she had never seen so magnificent a figure of manly beauty.

Richard glanced down at her with a proprietary smile. "We shall soon have our business settled," he advised her. "We'll arrive in Exeter in time for luncheon, and then stop by the Cathedral. After that," he raised his voice a little, "I shall require you to take Angela to a sempstress, Maggie, to commission some new dresses. Mr. Richard Bennet's wife must do him crrrredit in the deestrrrrict, ye ken!"

Maggie chuckled. She was not at all offended by his autocratic declaration, chiming in enthusiastically from the back seat with suggestions for the trousseau. Angela could not find it in her to register a dissenting voice to this chorus of happy anticipation, but contented herself with saying that she hoped the gentleman would deign to accompany them, since his earlier efforts in her behalf had been so successful.

Richard's eyes were at once diverted to the hat with the violets, and then to the small, sparkling face beneath it. He amazed his sister by agreeing to go with them to the dressmaker, on condition that they would solemnly promise that he himself would not be involved in any way except as Chancellor of the Exchequer.

For some reason, the picture of Richard Bennet involved with bolts of satin and cards of ribbon and lace, to say nothing of piles of corsets and female night-gear, so tickled Maggie and Angela that they went off into gales of laughter, at which Richard smirked like a precocious child who has amused his elders.

Thus the phaeton rolled through the lovely high-banked Devon lanes, sun-dappled, leaf-shadowed, accompanied by happy laughter. Angela, proudly seated at Richard's broad shoulder, felt she had never known such bliss.

The interview at the Cathedral passed too quickly for the dazed girl to retain much impression of anything but the twin Norman towers of the Church of St. Peter, a multitude of delicate spires, and a heavy yet benign face atop canonical garments. This important business was followed by two fascinating hours at the establishment of Miss Sarah Agnew, Modiste. After that, Richard took his exhausted but euphoric ladies to Mol's Coffee House, near the Cathedral. It was a fine old building, the front distinguished by enormous bay windows which glanced down upon the street through a myriad of shining small panes of glass. When they had mounted to the first floor, the proprietor proudly told them of the Elizabethan sea captains who had been wont to congregate in the bay of those very windows, drinking coffee or something stronger, and imagining themselves on board their own galleons, whose great cabins were similarly bewindowed.

It was a silent happy repast. Angela was scarcely conscious of what she was eating or drinking; it could have been ambrosia and the elixir of the gods, so sweetly did she savor it in her mouth. Richard glanced at her frequently, as though enjoying the ambience of her delight. Maggie watched both her young people with a complacent smile, but was wise enough to understand that small talk would be an intrusion upon that wordless communion.

On the trip home they maintained the comfortable quiet, and as the shadows lengthened, Angela's head nodded and drooped against the big shoulder beside her. Richard put his arm deftly around her, and settled her comfortably against him.

It was almost dark, and the tired horses had left the highway and were trotting along between the high banks of a lane toward the farm when disaster struck. Well aware that their stable, with its oats and cool water, awaited them, the horses had picked up their pace, and Richard had removed his arm from Angela's shoulders to better handle the reins. Maggie was collecting her parcels and checking her reticule. None of them was prepared for the attack when it came.

Four dark figures dropped down beside the phaeton from the high banks on either side. Two of them ran to the horses' heads, and caught at the bridles. The horses were tired, which probably explained why they did not panic and bolt, but permitted themselves to be held. At the same time, two other attackers leaped at the phaeton, one of them seizing Richard's arm and heaving out and downward while his companion struck at Richard's head with a short cudgel. The big man sank unconscious on the road.

While this was happening, too unexpected and well planned to allow for any defense, Maggie Bennet was peering through the gloom with alarm and swiftly mounting anger. Angela, asleep against Richard's shoulder, had first been suddenly bereft of her support and then roughly seized by a fifth man who had waited at the crest of the enbankment to observe the outcome of his careful strategy. When he saw Richard collapse under the cudgel blow, he scrambled down the bank and pulled the girl from the phaeton. At this, Maggie began to scream.

Angela's captor turned on his men with a snarl. "Get the farmer back into his phaeton." He turned to Maggie. "Old woman," he called, "can you handle the horses? Your friend is not hurt, I promise you. I am just collecting some-

162

thing which belongs to me. I mean you folk no harm."

"You are kidnapping my brother's fiancée, you skelpin! Release Miss Swann at once! My brother and she are to be married within the week!"

"Perchance he will not wish to marry her when he learns she is a thief—" The abductor interrupted himself. "Miss Swann, do you say? Where had you that name?"

"From the girl's stepfather, Gilles Loring of Swanholme," snapped Maggie. "It is not some hedge-bird you are abducting, young man! This girl is an heiress. You will sorely regret this night's work, you ruffian! I'll see you and your henchmen in the dock!"

At this threat, there were mutterings from the henchmen. Their leader tried to brazen it out. "I am Lord Merrel, old woman. The girl is an accomplice to the doxy who robbed me of a fortune in jewels. I wish only to question her."

"A likely story!" jeered the indomitable Maggie. "Do you tell me that, for a simple questioning, you must halt our carriage, like highwaymen, and knock my brother into the road—" This brought her attention back to Richard, still lying upon the road. "If you've killed him, I'll see you all hanged!"

Lord Merrel knew it was time to take firm action, before his men, recruited from among the younger grooms in his stable, and already

163

very uncomfortable with this act of derring-do, should panic and desert their master. Taking a firmer grip upon Angela, who had been silently struggling to be free, he commanded his men to heave Richard up to the seat of the phaeton and prop him against the padded back. When they had done so, he motioned them back to their horses, hidden over the crest of the bank.

"Away now, lads! I'll see ye at home."

Next he addressed Maggie, who had scrambled up beside the limp form of her brother and was chaffing his hands. "This girl has no doubt cozened you as slyly as she deceived me. I'll take her to my home and examine her, and if she can prove her claims of innocence, I'll release her at once."

"Richard and I," answered Maggie grimly, "will away to the magistrate and swear out a warrant against you, Lord Merrel! The girl is no cozener—she is an heiress! No," she interrupted, at his derisive gesture, "it was not from her lips that we had the information, but from those of her stepfather, Mr. Loring, who was here a day ago to discover if all was well with her, and to invite all of us to Swanholme, Miss Swann's ancestral estate in Cornwall. I would suggest that you go to him with your cock-and-bull story of stolen gems—"

Even in the failing light, Maggie caught the look of anguished appeal from the girl, and realized, too late, what she had done. Gilles

Loring would like nothing better than to see his stepdaughter accused of a crime. Even to let him know there was trouble would give him a perfect opportunity to take Angela firmly under his control again. And she had provided this raffish nobleman with Gilles's name and address! Maggie stared back at the girl in horrified awareness of what she had done.

Lord Merrel's gaze moved rapidly between the two faces. His self-confidence, which had been severely shaken by Miss Bennet's attack, was quickly restored by what he mistakenly interpreted as a look of guilt on the girl's face. Without lingering for further discussion, he swung Angela over his shoulder and scrambled up the bank. His carriage, with a team of four and a coachman and groom, waited beside the fence they had lowered to allow of their entrance to the field. Within moments Lord Merrel had hoisted the girl inside, joined her, and slammed the door. The coachman lost no time in departing the scene of what he privately characterized as some pretty havey-cavey doings.

Maggie Bennet was left in the dark furrow of the high-banked lane to care for the still unconscious Richard.

Chapter 13

ANGELA picked herself up from the floor of Lord Merrel's closed carriage and fell against the padded seat. With trembling fingers she smoothed her hair into order—her coronet-braid was unpinned and swinging down her back, and her hat with the velvet violets had disappeared in the struggle—and straightened her redingote. Then, taking a calming breath, she turned to the male figure slouched beside her in the gloom.

"Are you that Lord Merrel whose friend Zalie stole his jewels?" she asked. Although she was inwardly trembling with the shock of the sudden attack, she knew she must keep her wits about her lest Gilles Loring be called into the dangerous muddle.

Her companion only grunted. In point of fact, Julian Merrel was appalled at the outcome of his scheme, conceived over their brandy at the George and Horse by himself and his special crony, Sir Horace Tilling. Following the trail of a farmer called Bennet—not difficult, since he had written down his name and direction at the Pride of Exeter—they had discovered that he had in his household a young girl, a stranger to the district, whose position in the house was equivocal. Had they talked to Jonas rather than his wife, they might have learned that the dubiousness of the girl's role consisted of the fact that she was either housekeeper for Maggie Bennet or her guest. This had not transpired. On the basis of this incomplete information and two too many brandies, they had planned the exercise. It had seemed just the sort of reckless, dashing exploit which would set Julian up as a damned dangerous fellow when it was related, by Tilling, over the dinner table to his hard-bitten companions.

It had now assumed a more ominous aspect. Why the devil had he given the old woman his right name? If his damned groom had hit the farmer too hard, there could be unpleasant consequences. The host at the George and Horse hadn't had too much to say, but Mrs. Tilley had been loquacious about Richard Bennet when they were asking about the girl. She had praised the prosperous farmer who was a close friend of Milord Elsingham, the Great Man of the district. Could such a farmer really consider marrying this little chit beside him? The old hag had said so.

The trouble was that young Julian had rash

visions of himself as the very model of a bold Corinthian, a Buck of the first order. With the potent fumes of Jonas's brandy in his brain, it had seemed to be a wickedly dashing exploit. Now that the stimulating effect of the brandy had quite worn off, he realized that he was in for a splitting headache, and, worse, that he had in his carriage a female who might actually be the affianced wife of a landowner with important friends. In a very sour humor indeed, Julian told the wretched female to hold her tongue.

Angela was not to be discouraged. "I assure you, Lord Merrel, that the case is exactly as I told you in the Pride of Exeter. Your—friend Zalie, whom I met for the first time in the coach to London, fell into talk with me and persuaded me to break our tiring journey to dine and rest overnight at the inn. During the evening, she confided in me that she was fleeing from a distasteful marriage—"

"Fustian!" snarled Julian. "Surely you had enough *nous* to see that that was a Banbury tale? She got it at the theater the night before she robbed me."

Since the "Banbury tale" represented the exact truth of her own situation, Angela was momentarily daunted. However, her position was desperate, so she plucked up courage and went on, "She then suggested that we change costumes to confuse the pursuit—"

"Pursuit?" interrupted the man, roused by

this detail. "You were both running away from someone?"

"She said her father was forcing her to marry a man she hated," cried Angela, horrified that she had let him know she was in flight, also. "I could sympathize—"

But Julian was laughing harshly. "Zalie would have sold her soul for a wedding band!" He glared at Angela. "No female would rebel against a good marriage! You surely aren't gullible enough to believe that flummery?"

"Nevertheless, that is what she told me," persisted Angela. "I refused to change clothes as she suggested, since her garment was of a garish color and a style I could not admire. She told me you had chosen it, sir," she could not help adding waspishly. Then as Merrel leaned toward her menacingly, she hurried on. "When I awoke the following morning, in the tiny room we had shared, my own clothing was gone and Zalie with it. Perforce I donned her costume— which did not fit me at all, as you noticed!"

A wicked crow of laughter greeted that reminder. "Zalie's well endowed," the would-be Corinthian agreed.

"Well, I am not!" snapped Angela, resentfully, "and I would certainly not have wished to be caught in that very reprehensible garment! I went seeking Zalie, and got the information from the landlord's wife that she had taken the coach to Scotland. Did you fail to find her?"

"That should be clear to the meanest intelligence," sneered Lord Merrel. "Should I then be seeking her still—or her confederates?"

"Well, I am not one of such, as I have been at pains to tell you!"

"Continue your story!" commanded Lord Merrel, upon whose unhappy stomach the jolting of the carriage was having a very deleterious effect. His fear that further upset might cause him to shoot the cat held him to a more reasonable temper than he would normally have demonstrated. He opened a window. *"Well?"*

Thus adjured, the girl went on, "Mr. Bennet arrived to take me to his sister—"

Lord Merrel could not resist that opening. "Not very loverlike, was he? Almost seemed not to know you! Bit of a cold fish, is he? Pretty high in the instep, considering you was his intended, and he a farmer." The girl was dashed pretty with her great gray eyes gleaming at him through the gloom. Merrel tried to persuade himself that the girl's plausible tale was a complete fabrication, but his heart wasn't in it. Her speech was too well bred for a doxy, and her diffident little air of poise was exactly right for the person she claimed to be—a country heiress, not yet out into Society, rustic but of good family. Still, he thought, remembering Zalie's damnably persuasive wiles, she could be lying, and if she is, she's fair game. The idea aroused him in spite of the headache which was beginning to pound between his temples. He leaned closer to the chit and said again, "Is your precious Farmer Bennet a cold fish, my dear?" and placed his hand upon her thigh.

Angela drew away as though he had struck her. "Mr. Bennet does not display his feelings before a jostle of stableboys and strangers, if that is what you are implying!" she snapped. Then, to divert his thoughts from her person, she went on, in a cool voice, "The woman had a black leather case she seemed very careful of. I did not see what was inside it, so I cannot be sure she had your jewels, but she did rob me of my clothing, so I suppose I must accept that she robbed you as well. I went on to Bennet Farm that very morning, and have been there ever since, until today, when we drove into Exeter to obtain our special license from the Bishop."

"What sort of lying tale did you give the good cleric?" sneered Lord Merrel, but he admitted to himself that that cock wouldn't fight. He'd made a bad mistake, no question about that. He began to whip his befuddled wits, hoping to come up with some plan to save face. He was a hard-drinking, hard-riding, dissolute young nobleman who went about with a set of men of his own stripe, but so far he had confined his womanizing to soiled doves like Zalie, and had not been such a fool as to abduct a girl of good birth. So now, in a last-ditch stand, he asked,

"Did you tell the Bishop the same lies you told your farmer?"

Angela, unaware of his near-capitulation, was forced to accept the fact that the time had come for honest dealing. "I told him the truth, which you may verify by scanning the church records. I am Angela Swann, daughter of Denzil Swann of Swanholme, near Averly, and heiress to his estate. You have made a mistake, sir, but there is time to rectify it. Return me at once to Bennet Farm," she instructed. "If you do, and apologize to Mr. Bennet, I shall try to persuade him not to press charges—"

This last was the one word too many. Merrel had been searching for a way out of the mess he had gotten himself into, and would probably have decided upon some such notion as the girl had just proposed had she stopped after the announcement of her name and state. But when she suggested that her fiancé might be amenable to a simple apology after the foul blow he had received, Lord Merrel realized the girl was a complete innocent, overly optimistic, and foolish beyond permission—or she was lying about herself and the position she claimed. His suspicions were at once aroused. With rational thought addled by surly ill temper, disappointment, and the blinding pain induced by too much brandy, he committed an act of supreme folly.

Sticking his head out the carriage window,

he shouted at his coachman to head for home. "Forget about Tilling," he shouted. "Don't spare the horses!" Then, falling back against the squabs, he sank into a drunken stupor from which Angela's further requests and pleadings were quite insufficient to rouse him.

The coachman, taking comfort from the idea of a speedy ending to this disreputable enterprise, whipped up his team to such a pace that Angela dared not try to wrest open the door and fling herself out upon the road—a plan which had occurred to her. So, alternating between fear and trembling and surges of anger, the girl was racketed through the darkness toward an unknown fate.

The coachman gave no further thought to the abandoned Sir Horace. This did not matter, in the event, for that worthy was fast asleep in the best bed the George and Horse had to offer. In the morning he was quite unable to recall how he had got there, or even why he had come to this uninteresting village. Shrugging his shoulders philosophically, he took the next coach to London.

Chapter 14

WHEN Lord Merrel's coach arrived at his home just before dawn, there was surprise, alarm, and some scarcely smothered muttering upon the part of his less-than-devoted staff. The gist of it was that the silly gudgeon had cut some pretty totty-headed capers since inheriting his father's title and estate, as witness his loss of his mother's jewels to that light-skirt from London, but this kidnapping in plain daylight of some wealthy farmer's promised bride was the cap sheaf! They'd as like as naught have the Runners after them, if not a party of the injured man's friends bent upon reprisal. What was Master Julian up to? fretted his butler.

Julian Merrel was not up to much that morning after his ill-judged rape of the farmer's intended. Not that he had actually raped her, of course—he'd been too anxious to get away from the dangerous locality. Then, later, when his disapproving servants unloaded him from his coach, he was completely sunk in stertorous slumber.

On being advised in detail by the coachman as to the follies Lord Merrel had committed, the butler made stiff apologies to the young lady he had ushered into the drawing room. It was plain she was not one of Milord's usual light-skirts, for all she was sadly crumpled and bedraggled by the drive through the night.

"I am Blake, madam," he said soothingly. "Tea will be brought to you as soon as you have washed and refreshed yourself. May I escort you to Lady Merrel's suite? She is in London at the moment," and his expression added, *Thank God!* "She has been there with her sister since old Lord Merrel died."

"Then she has not yet heard of the theft of her jewels?" Angela nodded comprehension of the butler's anxiety.

"And I am hoping, Miss," Blake assumed a fatherly attitude, "that it will not be necessary for her ladyship to hear of *this* wretched business! Whatever can the resty young fool be thinking of?"

Angela did not find Julian Merrel's behavior exactly that of the foolish youth Blake was trying to present. She gave the loyal family retainer an old-fashioned look, and said firmly, "When I have tidied myself up and had a cup of tea, you may find me another coachman to drive me back to Bennet Farm."

It seemed she had not mistaken her butler. A sensible man, he disapproved thoroughly of his rakehelly young master, and was anxious to make up for his libertine behavior. Half an hour later, much refreshed by piping hot tea and a generous wedge of tasty beef and kidney pie, Angela smiled up at the hovering Blake.

"I think we both understand that Lord Merrel was—ah—under the influence when he brought me here this morning," she began in a voice whose calm steadiness rather surprised even herself. It would seem that her sojourn with the Bennets had helped her to strengthen her backbone. Blake was looking greatly relieved by her unhysterical acceptance of the situation.

"What would you wish me to do for the best, madam?" he asked, respectfully.

"Supply me with a vehicle and a driver."

"They are preparing a light coach for you now, madam. You'll be driven home at once."

"That is just as well," agreed the girl, thinking of Richard's temper at this moment. "Unless you are wishful of having a very angry Scotsman descending upon you. My fiancé," she added kindly.

"My God!" exclaimed the butler, forgetting decorum. "What's the silly fool been at this time?" But the question was rhetorical and they both knew it. Tom Coachman had spilled the whole tale, and Blake understood exactly what a coil Lord Merrel had gotten them into.

Within five minutes, a smart open phaeton appeared at the front door with a driver and groom up front. Blake assisted Angela tenderly into the rear seat, and spread a rug over her knees.

"I chose the open carriage, madam, in case you should encounter your Scotsman en route. I should not wish him to miss seeing you!" His tone was so apprehensive that the girl was forced to suppress a chuckle.

As the phaeton bowled along through the morning sunlight, Angela was glad of the rug, yet even the crisp air did not serve to keep her alert after her troubled night, and she was dozing off, propped against one side of the seat, when her eye was caught by the precipitate progress of a coach which was advancing toward them at a speed far beyond that commensurate with safety upon the King's Highroad. On the box, handling the reins with angry skill, sat a huge man with tousled sandy hair.

"*Richard!*" shrieked Angela, fearful lest this wild-eyed Nemesis should miss her as he raced past.

She need not have feared. Richard pulled his team across the road in a suicidal swerve, quite blocking the passage of the other vehicle, whose driver and groom had pulled up instantly upon hearing her cry. Angela was still struggling to disentangle herself from the rug when Richard, springing down from his coach and climbing up beside her, seized her in a fierce embrace which was strangely comforting.

He held her close to his big body for a long moment and then muttered harshly against her cheek, "You are safe? He did not hurt you?"

"He was in a drunken stupor the whole time," Angela assured her shining knight. "I am not sure he really knew what he had done."

Richard released her just enough to study her face sharply. Then the terrible tension began to relax in his body, and there was even the trace of a wry smile tugging at his lips. "You have just saved his life," he told her. "I had intended killing him as soon as I had rescued you."

"I think his potations of last night will be giving him his comeuppance this morning," Angela said. "Oh, Richard! I was so very worried about you! Is your head all right?"

"No thanks to Merrel," groaned Richard. "Now that I think of it," he grinned wryly at the girl, "I can only hope *his* head is giving him the same hell mine is giving me!" He touched the back of his cranium gingerly. "There's a lump here as big as an ostrich egg."

Angela took charge in the emergency, with all the new confidence she was discovering in herself. Turning to Merrel's apprehensive servants, she ordered crisply, "One of you can drive Mr. Bennet and myself back to the Farm in his coach. The other may follow in this phaeton and pick up his companion when we are through with him."

Richard's eyebrow rose quizzically, but he seemed content to allow his little love to arrange the matter to her satisfaction. Merrel's servants obeyed with a silent docility which rather surprised the girl. She allowed Richard to help her down and into his coach, and waited until the conscripted driver had them turned and rolling back along the road. Then she gave her rescuer a searching glance, to find his blue eyes fixed upon her countenance with equal intentness.

"Oh, my dear Richard," she said, and held out her arms to her battered hero.

He took her into his embrace and kissed her gently. At first she was reassured; then a little disappointed at the undemanding nature of the clasp. Pulling away slightly, she scanned the beloved features sharply. Surely, if he loved her, he would be more ardent at this moment?

Very much aware of her reaction, Richard confessed ruefully, "I really have the devil of a headache . . . and my eyes seem to insist upon crossing! Very odd! And so, my dearest dear, my *dear* heart, I think I had better try to rest . . . We have a great deal to do and to decide upon . . . but not . . . now is not . . ."

"Not the time," agreed the girl softly. "Dear Richard, would it help if you stretched out on the seat and put your head in my lap?"

Richard's dulling gaze brightened at this proposal. "I'm a wee bit too long for the seat, I'm afraid, but perhaps we might contrive something—"

"If you were to sit sideways," Angela found herself blushing but continued bravely, "and let me take your head and shoulders into my arms, I could perhaps cushion your head against the jouncing of this wretched road. . . ."

Richard swung around and presented his torso trustingly into her grasp. Angela was devoutly thankful that he had his eyes closed as she settled the beloved head against her breast and held him firmly, attempting fairly successfully to cushion him from the worst of the jolts.

"Your arms will cramp," murmured the man, settling against her bosom with a sigh of pleasure.

"I think not," she replied, as softly. "Rest, Richard, I shall not let you fall," and she braced her foot against the forward seat, the better to support his body with her knee. Then as he allowed his muscles to relax, she massaged the back of his neck with gentle fingers. Uttering a wordless groan of content, Richard slumped heavily against her.

Angela could have endured the effort of holding the beloved body if it had been ten times as heavy. She had a perfect chance to gaze upon his features, to trace with loving glance the strength and maturity of his face, now resting so trustingly upon her breast. She resigned herself to a long and possibly uncomfortable drive, but knew she would not willingly give up one minute of it. She wished she might stroke his face, but feared to rouse him from the sleep he needed. Instead she dreamed about the life of this fine, upstanding Scotsman who had made so strong a place for himself in the land of the Sassenachs. How could Lady Elsingham have refused him? she wondered. Yet it was obvious that that lady doted upon her own handsome husband. She left him free for me! exulted the girl. Loving her kept him from marrying someone else until I came! She found it in her heart to bless the lady.

I am besotted with this great creature, she thought, her glance running over the big body in her arms. His long legs were bent at the knees to accommodate their length upon the seat. Well-muscled thighs were propped against the rear squabs. One arm had managed, somehow, to insinuate itself behind her; the other was clasped loosely around the front of her body. Up to her nostrils drifted the faint warmth of his body. Angela kept up her soothing massage, loving the strong brown column of the man's throat. She thought that few moments in her future life would ever surpass the sweetness of this quiet reunion.

Chapter 15

WHEN they arrived at Bennet Farm late that day, Angela had to be lifted out of the coach, so stiff were her muscles from the long ordeal. Richard was dazed but cheerful as he was wakened and lifted out by two of his men. Maggie hovered, giving directions and cries of welcome at random. Within a very short time Richard, who seemed much restored by his sleep in Angela's arms, had dismissed the servants of Lord Merrel and sent them on their way with a gratuity. Then he and Angela were happy to accept assistance to their rooms and to let themselves be helped into bed with the minimum of fuss.

Angela was awakened next morning by Daisy, bringing tea and eager to hear of her adventures. She also told Angela that Dr. Grossgrain had been in to look at Richard, and after pronouncing him to be the greatest fool in Christendom for driving a heavy coach all night long with a cracked skull, told him he'd probably live in spite of his folly and the blow from Lord Merrel's groom.

Not excessively cheered by this Spartan diagnosis, Angela dressed hastily and joined Maggie in the dining room. "Is Richard really feeling more himself? Daisy tells me the doctor was not very reassuring," the girl said anxiously.

Maggie patted her shoulder. "Oh, Jem Grossgrain is a Job's comforter—never happy except when someone else is miserable," the old woman smiled. "Richard's sleeping peacefully now, and Jem says he should be up and about tomorrow morning as though nothing had happened to him." Her expression sobered. "That's not to say he won't be in a rare taking when he remembers what that monster and his servants did to you."

Angela nodded, her anxiety as great as Maggie's. "I hope he will be sensible and forgive them now he has me safe home," she said.

Maggie hugged herself at this indisputable evidence that the girl had accepted Richard, and herself, and Bennet Farm, as her true home and loving family. Maggie was a Romantic—as the Lord Elsingham and his Lady could have given witness.

In the event, Richard surprised both his well-wishers. Instead of anger he displayed a very

sober mood when he joined the ladies at breakfast the following morning.

"I have been thinking," he began, seriously,
having kissed both Maggie and Angela chastely
upon the cheek before seating himself, "that I
have been approaching this situation from quite
the wrong direction. So, as soon as I have discussed the matter with you both—for we Scots
are great folk for a democratic exchange of
views—I shall send a message to Lord Elsingham
telling him what I have decided. Then you and
I, my child, must prepare for a journey to Averly."

Although he was smiling provocatively at
her, Angela's heart fell at this statement. *Democratic exchange, indeed!* she thought forlornly.
*He has made up his mind to take me back to
Swanholme. He has discovered that he no longer
loves me!*

But Richard had not finished. "I believe we
shall find ourselves forever being subjected to
visitations from Loring and Merrel, and their
henchmen and dupes, if you do not return to
your own home, my good girl, and settle matters once and for all." He glanced at a sober-
faced Maggie. "You must admit I've the right of
it, sister. The lassie must take her stand. A
lecher like Merrel will never accept the truth
about Angela's lack of involvement in his affairs
until she proves that she is Denzil Swann's
daughter and the heiress of Swanholme. While
I cannot discover his Zalie or his jewels, I can

185

make sure that everybody from here to Averly knows that Angela Swann of Swanholme is no little hedge-bird, but the only daughter of a good county family. And that she is married to one Richard Bennet, who, while he may be a farmer, is able and ready to protect and care for his lady." He nodded once, hard-jawed and narrow-eyed. Both the women knew that there were few bold enough to challenge Angela's doughty defender.

"As for Gilles Loring," Richard continued, "we are all agreed, I take it, that that ruffian will try to wring every possible farthing from the estate of Swanholme. Which means he will continue to oppose Angela's marriage to me in every vicious way he can think of—"

"Oh, Richard, can I not sign it all over to him and be free of him?" pleaded the girl.

"You would give up your parents' home to this villain?" asked Richard sternly.

"Gilles has made it detestable to me," confessed the girl.

"I wonder what he has told your neighbors?" asked Richard. "For, believe me, such a fellow will have spread some ugly story to explain your disappearance. I must know what lies he has told about my future wife. I wish it to be possible for you to return to your family home without finding yourself befouled with Loring's innuendoes."

"He is right, Angela," pleaded Maggie. "You

must not allow your good name to be smirched by such a creature as Loring. You owe it to your mother and father."

Reluctantly, and with a deep sense of foreboding, the girl agreed to return to Averly and the house where she had been so brutalized.

The Elsinghams were informed of the delay and the reason for it, and agreed with Richard's plan. Their reception could be postponed until the return of the young couple from Swanholme. But Lord Elsingham advised against postponing the wedding.

"Angela will not be protected properly until she is beyond Loring's power to coerce," he said gravely. "I have set some inquiries in train as to his life before he appeared at Averly—"

"What have you found?" asked Angela eagerly.

"The report has not come in yet," Lord Elsingham admitted. "But I cannot believe, from his behavior to you and your mother, that he is a man of good character. I am positive we shall discover him to be a fortune hunter—if not worse." He looked at Richard. "I urge you to marry Angela as soon as possible."

But Richard had a bee in his bonnet and chose to disregard Lord Elsingham's advice. Maggie tried to explain his attitude to the troubled girl.

"He has his pride, Angela. He would not have it said that he had influenced a young girl unduly, or married her in some hole-and-corner fashion. Can you accept that?"

Although Angela accepted the decision without argument, she was disappointed and worried at what she felt was Richard's lack of enthusiasm for the marriage. If he truly loved her, surely he would not hazard their happiness upon what he himself would have called a chancy business—the visit to Loring in his castle?

Lady Elsingham was more successful than her husband in urging a course of action. "You may go to Averly unmarried, if such is Richard's decision, but you really must take Maggie to give you countenance. A fine thing for the maiden heiress to arrive out of the blue with a dashing stranger!"

Although they had all enjoyed a laugh, both Maggie and Angela insisted that Lady Elsingham was correct in her appraisal of the situation, and Richard gave way with his delightful smile.

Having declared himself so firmly, the big fellow was having second thoughts. Not that he felt he had made a mistake in his decision; no, it had been too carefully worked out in the quiet of a pain-filled night. But he had sensed a withdrawing, a coolness, in his little love, and, knowing himself to be the veriest tyro, an untried soldier in the battle of the sexes, he realized he would have to have a democratic discussion with the girl he loved. But the devil of it was that Maggie had turned a bit awkward, and was playing the chaperone as fiercely as though he were that lecher Merrel. *Maggie!* And Daisy was in it too, frowning and hanging about whenever it seemed there might be a chance of a private tête-à-tête with his fiancée. Richard, brooding on the strange ways of females when there was a wedding in the offing, made up his mind to proceed with *manly decisiveness.* That must be his rallying cry—his slogan!

To this end he approached Angela immediately after dinner that evening, when Daisy had just carried a tray of dishes to the kitchen and Maggie had followed her to see to the coffee. Richard rose swiftly and went to Angela's side.

"I wish to talk to you," he said with manly decisiveness. "At once. We'll go outside to our tree." Then he spoiled the whole effect by saying, with a wheedling smile, *"Please, Angel?"*

Angela, most flustered by the whole gambit, was so enchanted to be Richard's Angel that she rose without a word and let him take her hand and lead her from the room.

Congratulating himself upon his firm management of this important matter, the man led the girl out of the house and through the sunset fields to the great knoll crowned with its ancient tree. Having got her there, and facing the look of almost painful inquiry upon that beloved small face, his complacence fled and his throat seemed to close upon him. Finally he managed to get out a few words.

"Would you like to sit down?"

"If you wish, Richard."

This was going famously. Helping the girl to seat herself occupied enough time for Richard to marshall his thoughts, if he had been capable of doing so. Unfortunately, all the besotted fellow could think of was the jewellike beauty of her large eyes, the rosy flush of the sunset on her smooth cheeks, and the vulnerable sweetness of her soft pink mouth. This last thought quite unnerved the man, and he said, harshly, "I hope you do not think I am reluctant to wed you? The contrary is actually the case."

Angela's eyes opened even wider, and a delightful smile parted her soft lips. Richard grasped firmly at his self-control.

"I wish to wed you openly, in your own kirk, with the friends of your parents to witness the ceremony. I desire the whole district to know how proud I shall be to be your husband. Do you get my point?"

"Oh, yes, Richard!" sighed Angela, in such obvious relief and satisfaction that the man was quite compelled to take her in his arms and kiss that inviting mouth with manly decisiveness.

Several minutes later, surfacing breathlessly from the most agonizing bliss of his life, he glared down at the bemused girl in his arms.

"And that will show you," said Richard Bennet firmly.

"Yes, Richard," breathed Angela.

It was a perfect example of democratic discussion.

So, on the morning after the visit to Elsingham Manor, Angela set out on a return journey to the home from which she had fled, but this time she had big Richard Bennet as her champion, and Maggie Bennet riding behind them *en chaperone*. Still, Angela was not happy. She had a very real fear of placing herself in Loring's power again after she had so laboriously escaped him. Richard did not—could not—know how frightening the man was to her, how his long-practiced cruelties to her and her mother had bred in her a terror which was part loathing. She wished Maggie had supported her in her reluctance to meet her stepfather without the protection of Richard's name. But it was not for her to challenge the decisions of such a man as her intended husband. Long training had made it easy to accept the authority of a man, and when love was added, the conclusion was foregone. Still, the first day on the road, for all Richard's quiet good humor and encouragement, passed very slowly for the girl.

The second morning they were up betimes, enjoyed a superb breakfast at Turner's Inn, and set out on the road with spirits high. Richard expected to reach the village of Averly by evening, and had planned to put up at the Averly Arms for the night, to sound out the mood of the inhabitants and learn what scurrilities Angela's stepfather had spread abroad.

"For if we are registered at a public inn, no villain can put us away in some dark oubliette," he teased the girl. Angela tried to smile, but the feeling of looming misfortune was too strong. Even Maggie was beginning to wonder whether they had made a wise decision, as she saw the girl's face become hourly paler and more strained, and noted her white-knuckled tension.

It was late when they arrived, and they were led to their bedrooms by a yawning maidservant. Going down to breakfast the next morning, the first person they met was Mrs. Webster. She looked a little taken aback by the sight of the pallid girl in the modish new clothing—for Richard had insisted that she wear the clothes he and Maggie had bought for her at Exeter. The sempstress turned a welcoming smile upon Angela and took her timidly offered hand without hesitation.

The Bennets ranged themselves on either side of their charge. Angela hastened to introduce them. "Mrs. Webster, this is Miss Margaret Bennet, my hostess since I left Swanholme, and her brother, Mr. Richard Bennet of Elsinghurst Village, to whom I am to be married in

Averly church in a few days." She turned, blushing prettily, to her companions. "Mrs. Webster gave me the four pounds with which I was able to make my escape from Mr. Loring," she explained.

The Bennets made much of the dressmaker, their thanks warm and sincere. Mrs. Webster seemed greatly pleased by the encounter, and impressed by Angela's intended. She gave Richard a knowing smile.

"You're a better choice than that finicky fop of a nephew of Loring's," she commented. "Angela, does your stepfather know you're here?"

"We have not yet called upon him," stated Richard crisply.

"Perhaps I should warn you," began Mrs. Webster slowly, "that Gilles Loring has spread the rumor abroad that Angela took all her mother's jewelry and ran off with a dissolute nobleman and his doxy. He says he will not prosecute because of his respect for your natural parents, Angela, and will keep up his good stewardship of your estate against the day of your return, a blemished and broken woman, to the home you have dishonored." Her eyes twinkled as she recited the pompous platitudes in a voice meant to imitate Gilles Loring's usual style of public utterance. Two of her hearers were not amused. Richard was white with fury at these aspersions upon his future wife's character.

Angela was rigid with shock. Maggie startled everyone with a ringing laugh.

"How surprised good Mr. Loring will be when he finds the prodigal has returned, quite unblemished, to celebrate her wedding in Averly with her parents' old friends!" She beamed at the dressmaker. "I know I can rely upon you, dear Mrs. Webster, to spread the good news to all and sundry!"

"Why do you not go with Mrs. Webster, Maggie?" suggested Richard. "While she is introducing you to the 'all and sundry,' it will be a fine opportunity to spread the word and invite everybody in the village to our wedding. I shall commission our host here at the inn to provide a collation for everyone. That's after I've spoken to the minister. What's his name, Angel?" He took the girl's hand warmly in his, and gave her his special smile.

"The Reverend Quayle. He was Mamma's friend."

"Then he will be happy to see Mamma's daughter married to a man who values her," said Richard bracingly. "I'll see him now, and then we'll go to call upon your stepfather." He pressed her hand and delivered it to Maggie. "Wear your prettiest hat, love."

Angela was coaxed into a smile. Richard had returned to the sunken lane and recovered the hat with the violets from the bankside. It reposed securely in its own hatbox in her room at the inn this very moment.

Angela turned to Mrs. Webster. "Will you please come with Miss Bennet and me to call upon Mrs. Bothwell? She was my mother's dearest friend, and tried to help her just before she died."

Half an hour later, Richard was back at the inn calling for his carriage and handing Angela into it with a heartening smile and the whispered comment, "You are looking very pretty, Angel! Let us show that old skelpin that Denzil's daughter is worth two of him!"

Angela understood that Richard was trying to rouse her courage, but she would far rather have had him treat her as a beloved equal than as a timid child who saw a bogle behind every bush, to use some of his own phraseology. *Oh, Richard, you do not know what you are risking, either in challenging Gilles Loring or in offering to marry me!* The girl's spirits could hardly get lower, but she set her shoulders and kept a smile on her lips. She even pointed out interesting landscapes and pretty vistas as the carriage wended its way toward Swanholme—and Gilles Loring.

Chapter 16

DANVERS's eyebrows shot up as he opened the door to Richard and Angela. He stepped back nervously.

"Mr. Loring," requested Richard sternly.

"I'll just see if the master is free—" began Danvers.

Richard eyed him coldly. "You will inform him that Mr. Richard Bennet of Elsinghurst Village is here with Miss Swann, who will see him for a few minutes in the drawing room. Quickly now," he prompted, as Danvers seemed frozen to the spot, "we have much to do here in Averly to prepare for Miss Swann's wedding."

As Angela led her Scotsman into the drawing room, Danvers beat a hasty retreat.

Within three minutes the door shot open and Gilles Loring strode into the room. Instead of the consternation which Angela had hoped to see on his face, Gilles was grinning broadly. And just beyond him, face alight with leering laughter, came Lord Julian Merrel!

"You have come in good time to greet an acquaintance of yours, Angela!" Loring said gleefully. "Here is Lord Merrel come to tell me a most interesting story! We were, in fact, just leaving to call upon Sir Umphrey Long. Lord Julian intends to swear out a warrant for your arrest, my poor child!" he snickered.

"On what charge?" asked Richard quietly.

"On the charge of having conspired with that bitch Zalie to steal my family jewels," Merrel answered, with a wide grin. "I warned you, my dear! You really shouldn't have run away that morning before I was out of bed!"

"But you know I did not rob you!" protested Angela, her face pale. "I have explained again and again how it was!"

"Then you will have no difficulty in explaining once more to Sir Umphrey, will you? Perchance *he* might believe you!" sneered Loring. "No one else will."

Richard took the girl's hand and held it firmly. "Sir Umphrey Long is the local magistrate?" he asked.

"What's that to you?" mocked Loring. "Do you claim friends with him, also?"

"Why, I intend to go with you," replied Richard.

"For what purpose?" Loring blustered.

"I intend to swear out a warrant also—against Lord Merrel."

"What's this?" interrupted the young nobleman. Gilles shot him a lowering glance, which

198

did not miss Merrel's air of nervous discomfiture. From his heavy frown, it was obvious that the older man was beginning to have doubts that Merrel had revealed all the pertinent details of his meeting with Loring's stepdaughter.

It was Loring's turn to ask, belligerently, "On what charges?"

Richard was maddeningly devious and annoyingly Scottish in his reply to this challenge. "I had better warn ye, gentlemen, that I have already laid an information against yon lordling with oor own mageestrate, Lord Elsingham of Elsingham Manor. He has advised me that the beeesiness is a verra serious one—eenvolving, at the least, transportation—"

"*'Transportation'*? But that's absurd," began Merrel.

Loring interrupted ruthlessly. "On what charges, damn you?"

Richard appeared to be arranging a long list in his mind. "Stopping my coach upon the King's Highway; setting a band of hired bravos upon me, my sister and my fiancée; striking me down—that comes under the heading of 'assault and battery, with intent to do grievous bodily harm' by the way, Merrel, for which there is a very heavy penalty—robbery . . ."

"I never did so!" shouted Lord Merrel. "You know I only took the girl—"

"You kidnapped my fiancée. That is called

199

abduction," replied Richard. "The penalty for it is severe."

"You have no witnesses," protested Lord Merrel desperately. "Only this chit, who has a bad name in the district already, thanks to this old man's malicious tongue—"

"My sister is my witness. Miss Margaret Bennet."

"And who would pay any attention to a farmer's sister?" sneered Lord Merrel.

"I think Sir Umphrey might well do so, since Margaret Bennet is Lord Elsingham's old nurse, and is held in love and respect by Lord Elsingham and his wife. Shall we go?" and Richard tucked Angela's small, cold hand in the crook of his arm, and smiled at the two men.

"Danvers!" bellowed Loring, for once in his life giving way to panic. "Lock the front door and come here to help me restrain this madman!"

"It will be quite unnecessary for you and your minions to use force to restrain me," said Richard serenely, leading Angela over to a couch and seating himself beside her.

"Why do you say that?" demanded Loring. "Because you are outnumbered? We are three to one."

"It makes little difference," said Richard in a soothing manner which further enraged Loring. "Before we set out this morning, I had already told a number of people here in Averly that I have come to marry Miss Angela Swann by special license from the Bishop of Exeter. In fact," Richard grinned for the first time, "I rather think I have invited the whole village to attend the ceremony, and the reception at the Averly Arms which is to follow. Mrs. Bothwell and Mrs. Webster are busily distributing the invitations at this very moment." He nodded smugly at their dismayed expressions. "Yes, gentlemen—and I use the term loosely—the whole village knows that we are here with you. You cannot hope to hide our presence, or to conceal us in an oubliette!" He smiled at Angela. "When you are ready, my dear, we will go to swear out our warrants."

"I have already arranged with the Reverend Quayle to marry Angela to my nephew Vivian," blustered Loring.

"That is very interesting, sir, in view of the fact that you intend to charge your stepdaughter with grand larceny. Do you tell me that—er—Vivian is willing to marry a jailbird? Is he to wed her before or after she goes to jail?" Richard turned to face Lord Merrel. "As for you, sir, I should think you would be better employed in a search for your mother's jewels and your—friend Zalie, than in persecuting a young girl who has never done you any harm." His tone contained such icy disapproval that it brought the color up into Lord Merrel's cheeks.

"My stepdaughter is still a minor," protested Loring in a last-ditch effort to save the situation.

"I shall never permit her to marry you, you fortune hunter!"

"I shall be happy to prove, to anyone who has the right to inquire, that my circumstances are a good deal sounder than yours, Mr. Gilles Loring—if that is your real name," smiled Richard. "It might be pertinent at this time to warn you that Lord Elsingham has set in train an investigation into your background. He seems confident that we shall make some interesting discoveries."

Both men were staring at him with unconcealed alarm. Angela, forgotten for the moment, was regarding her champion with adoring eyes. Loring pulled himself together with an effort.

"Investigating me? Well, I'm prepared for that, young man! I'll just go to my study and get the papers that will tell Sir Umphrey all he wishes to know about me, and then we shall go to the magistrate together, to swear out our warrants!"

"I say!" gasped Lord Merrel, appalled at this betrayal.

Loring paid him no attention. With a tightish smile he went out into the hallway, closing the door softly behind him.

At once Richard was galvanized into action.

"Show me the way to the stables *quickly,* Angela! Is there a way from this room?" and he strode over to the French doors which led out onto a terrace.

"Yes! Follow me!" cried the girl, and ran before him through the doors and toward the rear of the house.

When they were in sight of the stables, Richard caught the girl's arm gently. "Thank you, love," he said. "Now return to the house at once. Get inside the house and stay there until I get this matter settled."

"Richard, you must not fight with him!" she pleaded. "He is brutal—vicious! He will not fight you fairly!"

"I have his measure," soothed Richard, patting her hand, his eyes on the stable. "Go now, my dear. At once."

Angela went.

Richard turned and ran lightly into the stable. He took up a position in a rear stall out of sight. He did not have long to wait. Within a few minutes he heard swift and stealthy footfalls. Peering over the edge of the stall, he watched a furtive Loring hastily saddling a horse. When he had it ready to ride, Loring strapped a small satchel behind the saddle. When Loring lifted one foot toward the stirrup, Richard strolled casually out.

"Going somewhere?" he asked.

Loring whirled with a curse, glared at the younger man, and then launched himself at his tormentor in a fury of frustration. He was a brutal man, and a vicious one, as Angela had warned, and he tried every dirty trick and low blow in his arsenal, but he found his rough-and-tumble tactics outmatched by the disciplined strength and skill of his young opponent.

For the first few minutes Richard was content to hold his own, testing out the angry man and gauging his power. Then he said, mockingly, "This is a little different from beating a dying woman and a young girl, isn't it, Loring?" and proceeded coldly to batter him to his knees.

Loring crouched, blood flowing freely from nose and lips, eyes reddening.

"Have you time for a second round before you run away?" jibed Richard.

Loring made no effort to get up, merely shaking his head dully, and resting on hands and knees. When it became obvious that he had no stomach for further punishment, Richard strolled over to the horse and removed the satchel from the saddle.

"I wonder what we have here?" he asked with a narrow smile. "Could it be the loot Angela was charged with stealing?" He broke the lock with his heel.

The satchel was packed with golden guineas, and in a little nest on top was a black velvet bag. Inside that was a tangle of flashing jewels.

"I imagine these belonged to Angela's mother," said Richard grimly. "I ought to kill you where you stand—oh, but you aren't standing, are you? Shall I find a whip and punish you as you deserve? Or shall I let you sneak away like the bullying coward that you are, and try to outrace the Runners?" He paused provocatively.

Loring stayed on hands and knees, refusing to face him. Richard moved closer. "You filthy, woman-beating—"

At this last, unbearable insult, Loring flung himself forward to catch Richard below the knees and topple him. But the crafty Scot had been warned. Lifting his knee in a crashing blow, he caught Loring in the face. The man went down in the dirty straw and stayed there.

There was a subdued murmur behind Richard. He whirled to face an admiring audience of grooms and stableboys. "You had better tend to your master," Richard advised them. "Get him ready for the Bow Street Runners." He scanned them carefully. "Miss Angela will be returning here, after her marriage, to decide what she wishes to do about her estate. Any of you who have—problems with the law would be advised to vacate premises while you have the chance."

The big man strode away, the satchel under his arm, whistling between his teeth.

Chapter 17

WHEN Richard strolled into the drawing room at Swanholme a few minutes later, he found Angela there alone, seated and looking anxious. His gaze was warmly intent upon her small figure.

"Has oor braw laird awa' an' left us, then?" he drawled.

Angela's wide eyes reflected the radiant smile which lit her face at sight of him. "Oh, Richard!" she said, without much originality or even relevance.

Richard, looking smug, seemed to feel that her comment was quite satisfactory. "Do you suppose you might find it in you to offer—er—aid and comfort to your champion?" he teased.

Angela tried to gather her scattered wits. She knew she was behaving like a moonling, besotted over this virile man with the devastating charm. Slowly, she got up and walked into his arms.

Richard bent his head, kissed her gently, and then grinned at her. "Satisfactory, under the circumstances," he said. "Loring is on his way, but before he left, he—returned some things he'd taken. Your mother's jewelry and quite a number of guineas," he explained. When the girl showed no interest in anything but his countenance, he quirked an eyebrow and pulled her into a closer embrace.

"My dear wee Angel," he said very softly, "I really canna promise to behave ma'sel' if ye perseest in giein' me that come-hither look! And what would the neighbors think, wi' us not to be hitched 'til tomorrow?" He kissed her with a fervor quite unlike the gentleness of his teasing. Angela gave herself up to the delight of it, responding with an ardent sweetness which brought a deeper glow to the Scotsman's eyes.

Fortunately for *les convenances*, there was a determined tattoo upon the front door knocker at this point. In a moment Danvers entered the drawing room to announce, "Mrs. Bothwell, Miss Bennet, the Reverend Quayle!"

Maggie pushed past him and hurried into the room. Then she saw Angela in Richard's arms. "Oh!" said Miss Bennet, and a wide smile replaced the grim expression upon her face.

Mrs. Bothwell also took the situation in at a glance. "So this is Angela's intended?" she asked. After one searching glance she too smiled widely. "Marian would be so pleased," she sighed.

The Reverend Quayle peered bewilderedly from the entwined couple to the ladies who had rushed him here so urgently. "I am not sure I quite understand," he began.

Reluctantly Richard took his arms away from Angela's soft, warm body. "I'm no' so sure I ken all the ins-and-oots ma'sel', sir," he said happily, "but och, man! it's a bonnie feelin'!"

"Richard!" rebuked Maggie. "This is the Reverend Quayle! I am sure you have something important to ask of him!"

But the Reverend Quayle, while conventional and not very quick on the uptake, was a man of learning and some wit. "How old are you, Mr. Bennet?" he asked mildly.

Richard turned startled eyes on him. "I'm thirty-two, sir," he said, and then, smiling, "Quite old enough to enter the holy estate, I assure you!"

"I was thinking of a comment of Dr. Samuel Johnson's, concerning Lord Mansfield, a Scotsman educated in England," the Reverend Quayle elucidated with scholarly relish. "He said, 'Much may be made of a Scotchman, if he be caught young,'" and the good cleric beamed at their delighted laughter.

"Ay, Ah'm caught for sure," gloomed Richard. "There's naught for it but to get leg-shackled this very day! Since Ah was persuadit to secure a special license, an' a' that, Ah canna see hoo Ah'm ta wiggle oot!"

Angela put a small, possessive hand on his arm. "I shall never let you get away, Richard," she said adoringly. "You are my true knight."

"Och, the lassie's daft!" chuckled the big fellow, taking her back into his arms to the satisfaction of all beholders. " 'Tis plain some body must take care o' the puir bedazzled girl—and I canna permit anyone but masel' to do the task properly!"

Chapter 18

AND so they were married, Richard Bennet and his Angel, in the little church which had seen the marriage of Denzil Swann and Marian. The ancient building was packed. Latecomers were clustered around the doors and at those windows which were not glazed with stained glass. Maggie Bennet, a small sturdy tower of strength, unexpectedly elegant in silver-gray taffeta, stood beside Angela. At Richard's shoulder, Lord Elsingham acted as his neighbor's best man, and the beautiful Lady Elsingham adorned the pew set aside for Friends of the Groom.

Thanks to a determined—and delighted—Mrs. Webster, Angela was a dream bride in white silk and lace which clung gently to her softly curved young body. Mrs. Bothwell had requested permission, gratefully given by Angela, to search among the boxes in the attics at Swanholme for the veil which Marian had worn for her wedding. It was exquisitely beautiful, and fell softly over the bride's shining dark hair. It also served as a screen to protect Angela from the curious or critical stares which she dreaded. Gilles Loring's venom had been spread widely in the district, and the girl feared there might be many who would condemn such a contemptible creature as he had made her out to be.

She need not have worried. Richard and Lord Elsingham had visited the local squires in the three days before the wedding, explaining Loring's defalcations and subsequent flight at the threat of the investigation Lord Elsingham had set in train. With the hasty departure of Gilles and most of his servants, the good folk of the district were eager to admit that they had had their suspicions of Loring. The men especially showed themselves resentful of Gilles's deception. Even a few high sticklers, who had been heard to declare themselves unwilling to give countenance to that runaway female and her farmer, persuaded each other it was their social duty to prove to the Elsinghams that not everyone in the neighborhood was as ramshackle as the Swanns and Loring. Added to this, Mrs. Bothwell and Lady Elsingham made a powerful duo of sponsors for the girl whom most people began to remember as a charming child.

When Angela had visited her mother's grave the day before the wedding, she had been surprised and deeply moved to find it decked with beautiful blossoms. She accepted the gesture gratefully as an acknowledgment of regret for the unhappiness Marian Swann had suffered with her cruel second husband.

But today, looking up through her filmy veil at the huge, sturdy Scotsman beside her, Angela felt a surge of pure joy so powerful that it made her dizzy. She would do her utmost to make him happy. If only she knew what he wanted of her ... but surely he would instruct her? She smiled up at Richard with such sweetness that he caught his breath, and the hand which held hers tightened and then trembled before he released her own small palm.

At this point Richard, who had discovered what he had to do from a most reliable source, launched into his carefully planned program. As his mentor beamed sentimentally from her excellent vantage point in the first row, Friends of the Bride, position, Richard bent, lifted the delicate veil with reverent fingers, and taking his new bride into his arms with manly decisiveness, possessed himself of her lips.

Angela, who had not had the benefit of professional advice on ceremonial behavior, at first widened her eyes in surprise and then dropped her eyelids and accepted blissfully the pressure of Richard's warm, firm lips with reciprocal enthusiasm. Richard had not counted upon the effect of this cooperation. His own eyes, half closed in pleasant bemusement, shot open as wide as Angela's had originally done, and then sought the admiring gaze of Mrs. Webster with some alarm.

"Surely not in front of the whole congregation?" his startled glance seemed to inquire.

Mrs. Webster's nod reassured him, and marveling at the license of this permissive age, Richard Bennet settled in for a pleasant interlude. A certain restiveness in the congregation finally brought him back to earth, and he released the girl reluctantly and turned her to walk up the aisle with him.

Mrs. Webster wiped a tear of pleasure from her eye as she recalled the visit this fine upstanding fellow had paid her the previous day.

"I have come to thank you for your goodness to Angela," he began.

When Mrs. Webster protested that she devoutly wished she had had enough sense to do more for poor Mrs. Loring and for Miss Angela when they were so desperately unhappy, Richard told her he had heard of her quick thinking in providing paper money the girl could conceal about her person, which enabled her to make her escape from the intolerable situation in which she found herself.

"It is plain to me that only your good self, Mrs. Webster, and Old Beamish, did anything at all to help my dear lass in her desperate plight, and you have my undying gratitude for it!" He collected his poise and continued in a less fervent tone, "You will understand why I do not intend to take our honeymoon at Swan-holme. Angela's birthplace has become a place of torment to her. In time, I hope that those dark memories will fade, and she will wish to revisit Averly. In the meantime, Lord Elsingham is providing us with the services of one of his own men as bailiff of the estate. He will hire staff enough to keep the house and property in good heart. But it was not," Richard went on, touching an immaculate handkerchief to a fore-head obviously moist, "to weary you with such tedious business that I requested this inter-view, Mrs. Webster, but to consult you as a dear friend to Angela upon a—" he held onto his calm with an effort, "—a delicate matter."

The admiring female, already under the spell of so much braw Scottish manhood and charm, was understood to say that she would be hon-ored to assist Mr. Bennet in any way.

Relieved at this first hurdle successfully nego-tiated, the man gave her his best smile. "You must be aware that I am no London Beau, full of *nous* and worldly knowledge. I need help, ma'am! I would not frighten or disgust my darling girl. Can you tell me how young women wish a new husband to behave?"

Mrs. Webster's mouth fell open and she was momentarily deprived of speech.

Richard did not seem aware of her surprise. He continued, frowning soberly, "I would not wish Angela to be deprived of any distinguishing notice or customary attentions, but you must understand I have been a guest at very few weddings, and while there, have paid too little heed to those small details which might be valued by—by the bride." He smiled tentatively at Mrs. Webster. "I should like to make the occasion a perfect one for Angela—and I am not sure, that is . . ." for all his determination, Richard was running out of courage.

Mrs. Webster, rapidly recovering from shock, said a little vaguely, "Oh, *those* details," and made haste to supply him with as much information as her romantic nature could provide. "Well, first, you must turn to look at her as she comes down the aisle to the front of the church," she began. "It is not properly done, but shows you are so eager to see her that you defy convention."

"Do you tell me there are bridegrooms who do *not* turn to make sure the girl is coming?" marveled Richard. "I should not wish to miss the sight of Angela at such a moment!"

Mrs. Webster agreed heartily. "Then, at the end of the ceremony, you must lift the veil and kiss her—"

"In front of everyone?" demanded Richard. "This is acceptable in the kirk?"

Mrs. Webster brushed puritanical notions aside airily. "The kiss must not be too short, or perfunctory, lest it indicate that you really are not pleased with your new wife. On the other hand, it should not be so lengthy or ardent as to embarrass the guests—or the bride."

Richard dutifully took out a small notebook. "How long would that be?" he inquired practically. "Is there a rule?" Then he grinned. "I had better warn Lord Elsingham to give me a nudge, for if I'm left to my own devices I may forget to stop."

Pleased by, but correctly ignoring, this levity, Mrs. Webster went on, "Then there is the reception, afterward," she said, warming to her task. "You'll be expected to stay near her, see that she gets some nourishing food to give her strength for—that is, see that she eats." She hurried on, trying to ignore the devilish twinkle in Richard's eyes. "You'll be expected to answer the toast to your bride, and have a couple of easy phrases prepared to thank all your well-wishers as they go past you to offer their congratulations. Usually just *thank you*, or *you are so kind*, or *so good of you to come*, will suffice. After all, one does not expect a bridegroom to be making fulsome speeches."

All this was being jotted down in Richard's notebook. "How long do we have to dawdle about—that is, what is the usual length of the reception? Should I not be showing some manly eagerness to bear off my prize?" And again that devilish twinkle delighted his mentor.

"You must remain at least until everyone has eaten and has had a chance to offer you congratulations," she advised him. "Then you slip away and change into traveling clothes, and meet your bride in the front hallway—in this case, at the front door of the inn—where you receive final good wishes as you enter your carriage and drive away."

"I think I can manage that," mused Richard, eyeing the woman speculatively. "You have been so kind, Mrs. Webster, and I am deeply grateful. There's just one thing more. Can you tell me anything I should know about what a woman expects of a new husband, for och! I'd like fine to make it a perfect time for my Angel." Dark red color was in the man's cheeks, and his eyes, though steady on hers, were almost glazed.

Mrs. Webster stared at him, torn between embarrassment and admiration. At length she said quietly, "With the care you have shown that this should be a happy experience for Miss Angela, I am sure you'll make a gentle and loving bridegroom. Bless you, Mr. Bennet— follow your heart's prompting! I'm thinking Angela is a lucky girl."

With this encouragement, Richard took his leave of his kind mentor. "I was all about in my head to think the village sempstress could instruct me," he told himself, "and I'm damned if I'll ask Lord Elsingham! So, Angela darling, I'm afraid you'll have to put up with a novice at this most important time—and we'll both do our best to make it perfect. I've no doubt it may

218

take practice!" And at that provocative thought, the man grinned with sudden delight.

It seemed to Richard, the next day at the inn, that the wedding reception would never end. So many of the important families had come to hobnob with the Elsinghams, and they offered so many toasts to Denzil Swann's daughter, that Richard was afraid he would be too tipsy to drive his bride to the place he had in mind for their honeymoon. But at length the last toast was offered and honored, the goodies demolished, and the musicians persuaded to abandon classical airs and play melodies suitable for dancing. The older folk were ready to withdraw. Angela had been helped to change by Maggie and Mrs. Bothwell. The latter now took her leave with a warm kiss upon the girl's cheek. Maggie came to stand before her new sister-in-law.

"My dear," she said gently, "I canna think of any woman in the world I'd rather welcome to our family than your sweet self. Make him a loving wife, Angela, for he's a good man and will hold to you all the days of his life." She hugged Angela and went quietly ahead of her out the door.

Looking enchantingly pretty in her violet hat and a traveling dress in the same soft color, the gift of Mrs. Webster, Angela went down the stairway to the front hall. She could see Richard standing by the open door, very dashing in his skintight buckskins and a coat as blue as his eyes, and beyond his rugged form the outline of the shining curricle with two dapple-gray horses. As he caught sight of his new wife, Richard's face broke into a wide, involuntary smile, and his blue eyes sparkled.

Then they were out the door in a flurry of good wishes and flower petals—a charming idea of Lady Elsingham's. Richard boosted his wife easily up into the seat and tucked a light robe over her knees. Then he mounted beside her and took the reins from the grinning hostler. With a final wave, they were away.

Angela caught her breath. "Maggie—Is she not to come with us?"

"On our honeymoon, my dearest Angel? I do not think it is quite *comme il faut*," teased Richard.

Angela, blushing, cast a sideways look at him and was, as had become her wont, quite overcome at the manly beauty of his face and figure. After a small silence she asked shyly, "Where do we go, Richard?"

"We are going home, Mrs. Bennet," her husband told her. "Since I expect us to live there for the rest of our lives, I would like to make the place pleasant and attractive to you. And I cannot imagine," he said softly, "a more wonderful memory to beautify our home than that of our honeymoon. We shall be quite alone in the house. Maggie is to be a guest of the Elsinghams at the Manor; Daisy and the other maids will stay with their parents, and come in only when we send for them to clean the house and make our meals. Of course *I* shall make your breakfast every morning."

This pronouncement served its purpose of making Angela laugh. "Can you cook?" she asked, a little breathless at the thought of being alone with Richard.

"Do you doubt it?" teased her husband, and then, sobering, he reached out and caught her hand in his big one. "Oh, Angela, my very dear," he said softly, "I want so much to be alone with you! Is that what you wish also, my wife?"

Her cheeks ablaze, the girl met his eyes steadily. "Yes, dearest Richard, I want it above all things."

"You will not be afraid?" questioned the man.

"Of *you?*" Angela smiled at him.

Richard caught his breath at the radiance in her face. After a pause he said, "I hope I can wait to get you home. I want so much to hold you in my arms—very close."

"Yes," agreed Angela. "Oh, yes!"

By dint of pushing the grays very hard, and not stopping for a dinner which neither of them wanted, the newly wedded couple reached Bennet Farm before midnight. Richard, relinquishing the reins to a welcoming groom, led his bride to the front door of the moonlit house.

"Now I carry you over the threshold of your new home, my bonny dear. It is the custom."

Angela lifted her arms and clasped them around his neck as he caught her up against his broad chest. A lamp burned in the hallway, and the house welcomed them with the scent of flowers.

Kicking the front door shut behind him, Richard carried her up the stairs to his bedroom, where again flowers sweetened the air. "Are you hungry? Shall I make you some tea?" he asked as he set her on her feet by the great bed.

"No, thank you, Richard. I—I am tired."

"Too tired, my love? Would you prefer I did not make love to you tonight? I would have our first time together to be perfect for you."

Angela looked up into his beloved face with honest eyes. "To be with you is what I wish for. I dote upon you, Richard. I am in your hands."

The man laughed joyously and came to stand beside her. He took her firmly into his arms. "Once I said that with your innocence and my abstinence, it was as if the blind led the blind. But you, my own true love, have given me my sight." He kissed her with tenderness and passion, then lifted his head and regarded her glowing little face with the wicked twinkle she adored in his bright blue eyes.

"Beloved," he said, "I must tell you I have been giving this matter considerable thought. It has occurred to me that our First Ancestors could have had no rules to follow, no precedents to guide them, no manual of instructions. And what Adam could do, a Scotsman can surely do as well!"

"Better, I am sure!" affirmed Richard's Eve, and gave herself into his adoring embrace.

Let COVENTRY Give You
A Little Old-Fashioned Romance

☐ MISS KEATING'S TEMPTATION   50226 $1.50
by Margaret SeBastian

☐ A FRIEND OF THE FAMILY   50227 $1.50
by Denice Greenlea

☐ THE HEIRESS COMPANION   50228 $1.50
by Madeleine Robins

☐ DELSIE   50232 $1.50
by Joan Smith

☐ MISS MIRANDA'S MARRIAGE   50233 $1.50
by Claire Lorel

☐ THE SUN WITH A FACE   50234 $1.50
by Meriol Trevor